A Blue Coast

Mystery

Almost Solved

Nick Sweeney

A Blue Coast Mystery

Mystery

Almost Solved

Addison & Highsmith

Addison & Highsmith Publishers
Las Vegas ◊ Oxford ◊ Palm Beach

Published in the United States of America by
Histria Books, a division of Histria LLC
7181 N. Hualapai Way
Las Vegas, NV 89166 USA
HistriaBooks.com

Addison & Highsmith Publishers is an imprint of
Histria Books. Titles published under the imprints of
Histria Books are distributed worldwide exclusively
by the Casemate Group.

Library of Congress Control Number: 2020937915

ISBN 978-1-59211-064-3 (softbound)
ISBN 978-1-59211-069-8 (eBook)

A Blue Coast Mystery

Mystery

Almost Solved

To Brendan Cassin, who taught me
the value of a story
and
To Michael 'Red' Reece, who told me
a few tales

I knew this junkie in the mid-seventies, when I worked in St. Giles Hospital in Camberwell, South East London. He was there because of malnutrition and general neglect, and not for treatment for drug abuse, and every time he was discharged, I knew it would not be long before he was back. I also knew that, one day, he wouldn't make it. I knew him as much as you can, or want to know junkies if you're not one, and even, I suppose, if you are. His name was Henri, pronounced as in French, though there was really nothing French about him.

In response to a locum who asked questions that made plain his disapproval of junkies, Henri said quietly, "I'm not into debating things that ought to be clear to people who claim to be intelligent." I stifled a laugh. The locum did too, to be fair. I caught a brief wink from our bed-bound junkie, who then settled down for the mid-morning nap that countered his usual sleepless night, his veiny arms outside the sheet, his bitten nails neat and pink. I wagged a naughty-boy finger at him, before catching up with the locum on his round.

Henri's whole life wasn't in St. Giles, of course. Nor was it in the streets of Camberwell, where I'd see him occasionally whenever he was discharged. He never seemed to stray far from St. Giles, as if he wanted to keep the place in sight, just to be safe. I watched him, noted his collar askew, one trouser leg shorter than the other, the scrappy end of a scarf sticking out of one sleeve, as if he'd dressed in a hurry in somebody else's clothes. I saw him affect affability as he asked people for money. Though haggard, haunted even, he never quite acquired the patina of the tramp, nor the patter of the beggar, being too long-winded, and too diffident. People who donated despite this were rewarded with a look of fake gratitude. It was fake, because, after a certain point, nearly everything a junkie shows the world is fake.

"Even my name is fake," he told me. I'd guessed as much, but didn't care what name he wanted to use. The one in our hospital records was good enough for me, and anyway, I couldn't be doing with the bother of changing it. That was the first time I bought him a cup of tea, in Nick's, a café near Camberwell Green. "This is real." Henri held up the tea. "But what made you buy it for me is fake." I was too tired not to agree. "But because the tea is real, and the cup, and the money you paid for it, then it doesn't matter. As long as some of the... thing... the process is real." He looked into my eyes, his own alive, searching.

He talked in that almost-intellectual way to seem enigmatic, I suppose. He never quite managed it, and in any case it was a bore, no longer clever now that it had appeared on the television, first in deadly seriousness, and then, already dated, sent up in satire. I suppose Henri didn't realize that, as he had no television, or so I assumed; he couldn't know that the world had caught up and become as clever as he had once been. I was tetchy, perhaps – I'd usually been up all night on shift whenever I met him – and said all this. Something changed in his face, a flare of anger replaced by acceptance in such a quick turn-around that I thought I'd imagined it.

I continued to call him Henri, with the accent on the second syllable. "Henry just sounds... wrong to me now," he said. "Plodding. From a time before the war."

"True." I had to laugh.

"I'm from before the war, of course." In those days, people who said that meant the Second World War. If his date of birth wasn't fake too, then this was true, by a year. It was impossible to tell his age from his look; his teeth were ruinous, and his hair, though dark, with a hint of metallic grey, was straggly and thin, and fine lines had dug a way into his face.

I'm mostly Irish, and partly Catholic, and I'm not religious, but I sometimes thought of Henri as living in a sort of purgatory; Camberwell was just a stop along the way to his real destination, wherever that might be. Because of that, our surroundings didn't seem to be very important to him. Whenever we went for those cups of tea, and the occasional breakfast if it was the right side of pay day, Henri told me part of his story.

Early on, he told me that he had been born in Boston, the one in Lincolnshire, but, as if the subject bored him literally unutterably, he stopped the autobiographical details there. He fast-forwarded twenty five years through schools, playmates, sports, university, jobs, girls, and pubs to the nineteen sixties, when he lived on the French Riviera. It was a place I knew by proxy, through the fascination with it in James Bond films, and then spoofed in one featuring comic duo Morecambe and Wise.

Somewhere between Boston and the Blue Coast, Henri had got himself a countess – one from a strain of French aristocracy left un-beheaded in the Revolution, but a real one, all the same. I never got much of a picture of her, just a stark outline revealing that she was a junkie too – how else could it have been? She introduced Henri to the fringes of the Rolling Stones' tax-exiled circle from a connection with her dealer, a guy called Jean who had been Marianne Faithfull's beau, and sometimes still was. "My countess was what they call chic," Henri said. It was the first time I'd heard that word, and he had to explain it to me. "Part of this sort of… beau monde – beautiful scene," he translated further. "But up close, it often wasn't so beautiful."

They were welcomed in to Keith Richards' mansion in Villefranche sometimes, by Keith's vigilant girlfriend, Anita Pallenburg, but at other times shooed out of it, when she wanted to remind everybody that the party, for a time at least, was over. Henri dropped the names, but only as background to his tale; he claimed that his life was uninteresting, even with the Stones in it, and, in any case, a bit of a daze. Perhaps he was that joke come true: if you'd truly lived through the sixties, you wouldn't be able to remember it. That sixties story had been told so many times by then, and at tedious length, by chroniclers and documentary-makers, using a lot of faces prettier than Henri's to populate it, and he seemed happy to wash his hands of it.

Two

Henri told me another story. It was about a couple who were almost the opposite of anybody in the Stones' entourage; they were from a world long before the sixties, and yet lived in one that existed both in and out of that mad decade when it was felt that anybody could become whoever they wanted to be. This couple didn't seek fame, but the shadows. They were artists, but didn't seek to leave art behind as a monument to themselves; their art was nightly, ephemeral edifices made by sleight of hand, a certain finger placed in a certain way on certain small items – a lighter, for example, or a wedding ring – or the barest twitch of an eyebrow: they were a pair of Blue Coast card players.

They were among a paradoxical minority on the coast: transients who managed to live there almost all their lives, and yet still not be fully of the place. The seasons changed the make-up of their lives, and of the memories of them that others took away, but kept them there, each year a little greyer, a little more faded, and a little poorer.

People remembered the couple living in an Art Deco ruin of a hotel near the Paillon river, and in a draughty bungalow by the cemetery under Haut Cagnes, in an apartment described as needlessly sumptuous over the flower market, and in a suite at one of the fancy hotels almost on the promenade. They were never at these places for long, and they told Henri they remembered little about them: the dwellings were incidental to the act of living.

The last was a two-roomed cold-water apartment in the suburbs of Nice, over a car repair shop, a business run by an old man called Villemont who, it was rumored, had 'done well out of the war'. He was wiry, his hands always active, clenched, his pale eyes unflinching, challenging all to dare ask about that period of his life when the Nazis terrorized his country. He was traditional in his ways; he didn't employ anybody but family, and didn't encourage his workers to dawdle around the place, wouldn't let it become a hangout for aimless young men. He believed in a siesta in the summer months, and in knocking off at the advertised times.

Villemont was sometimes heard to say that he didn't like the tenants above him – and he didn't have to, did he? – but tolerated them because they were quiet, and caused no trouble, and because, as a businessman, he understood how hard it was for Adie, the landlord, to rent out a place over a car repair shop. He didn't like Adie much, either, but at least they shared the chasing of an honest franc.

Out front there were trees to hide both the sun and the apartment blocks across the narrow street. Out the back, a slope led to a vacant lot that, unbuilt on, had lapsed into use as a dump. It was full of abandoned bedsteads, cookers, furniture, bicycles, cars, even, at least one truck, and other cast-offs from modern life, gravitating towards a pool that grew and shrank, that imitated metal, went between the colors of lead and rust. It was a leak from below, perhaps – water supply pipes, or, worse, sewage outlets – replenished by the storms that lashed the coast in the winter, the ones the tourists never saw. The harsh environment stopped neither the shrubs that grew between the rusting hulks of consumerism, nor the birds that perched on them and sang, the dogs and cats that played on them nor, once, a mysterious grey monkey from who-knew-where – a zoo, a circus, or a ship, most likely, abandoned to a fate people could only guess at. "If you could ignore all that," Henri said, "you had a view – what they call the Bay of Angels, the blue sea, this... mad deep blue like the one kids draw with crayons at school, and a big blue sky like you never see here. Man it was something."

The couple Henri told me about lived in a city in which, it might be said, they stuck out, but in fact they were surrounded by odd people, in the nearby rows of apartments reclaimed and restored after the war, but already shabby, and in need of attention. Those people were not exactly secretive, but generally kept their thoughts to themselves. They said good morning neutrally, like diplomats, or gravely, in the manner of pessimists.

All such people liked the way the city teemed around them and closed them in. "Some people fear the open spaces," the man from the couple said to an idler in a seafront café, a tourist he would never see again. "And seek the sanctuary of streets, no matter how dirty, or mean." That piqued the interest of another idler, a certain junkie who was unerringly British and yet, already, had adopted an undeniably French name: our Henri, destined eventually to haunt not just the Blue Coast, but Camberwell's streets and cafés, and its almost-famous patch of grass, its bath-house, its hospital dedicated to obscure St. Giles, and its Tiger pub, where my mum worked behind the bar.

"It's funny to think," Henri said to me, years later, "that I'd probably never heard of Camberwell at that point in my life. Villefranche-sur-Mer was more familiar to me, and its characters."

"Mmm." I saw his streaky eyes, the gaps in his teeth, the dry skin around his nostrils, and caught a whiff from his raggedy clothes. I must have been feeling particularly cranky that morning. I nearly imitated his pronunciation, to say, ooh – soor meyur – very fancy, but said anyway, "Except not so funny now, eh?"

What could I have meant? The rain outside, I suppose, the grim, grey-faced kids trudging to school, the old woman who looked like she'd strayed out of a Charles Dickens book, muttering in the corner, the early-morning drinker who'd once told me at St. Giles that black worms came out when he tried to urinate, the tabloid-reading builders who were swearing loudly about nothing. Those were the characters Henri was stuck with, now. That was... probably what I meant. The moment was vivid: me with my chin on both hands. I didn't know whether to be pleased or depressed when Henri answered me, "No. Not so funny," and yet still dived back into his story set on the French Riviera.

When Henri first got talking to the card-playing couple, the man intoned Henri's name carefully, on the verge of friendly mockery. Henri was another tourist they would see that one time only, they supposed, but then they ran into him again, and again, and recognized him as a fellow-outsider. His life was a wreck, they noted, but saw that he was not resigned to it in some miserable way. It seemed that they approved of people who embraced their fate with dignity.

All the same, the man felt a little sorry for Henri. He had smoked the odd pipe of hashish, but he couldn't make out why anybody would fill his mind with an everyday narcotic – get up in the morning and turn his waking mind into a dreamscape – the torture of it: why would a man do that to himself?

Only after they became friends, and he was able to ask Henri this to his face, was he able to confess that he had his own dreamscape. He and his companion had been counting cards in their sleep for more than thirty years, and were now catching sight in their waking moments of those hearts, diamonds, clubs, spades, numbers and the haughty royal faces of kings and queens, the mocking ones of knaves, and the ivory ball that brought fortunes or made them vanish with the silence following a final click.

They didn't always talk to Henri, but he was often in the background, cheerful, slightly ragged, slightly wrecked, as they told parts of their stories to countless ten-minute acquaintances. In this way, Henri learned that the man did indeed avoid those open spaces, carrying deserts in his head as well as card trickery, grainy films of his people forced to march under merciless suns, at the mercy of those with no mercy to offer, from Ottoman pashas up on high to the lowest mountain peasants. Henri had barely heard of Armenians, but they took gradual shape in his head, courtesy of his new acquaintance, their fate to be marched out into an eastern nothingness, and starved, or forced into the Aegean Sea in the west, to drown, and be forgotten by the world.

Not long after he first spoke to them, Henri woke from a heroin stupor and said to his equally stupefied countess, "I know them." She didn't know who he was talking about. "Well, not... know, exactly." Nor did she care who he was talking about, particularly. He walked around, talked to the room about seeing the couple in the crowds awaiting the end of a bicycle race on the Promenade des Anglais the year before. He recalled their faces clouding over as the winner crossed the line. It was their cue to tear up their betting ticket stubs and turn away, suddenly untouched by the spectacle, and the bonhomie and hubbub around them, their moment soured by loss. "But even then," he told the countess, "they had a kind of... elegance."

"Who?" she asked him.

And he remembered them from another occasion, just walking – no, promenading, a matter of style, not just seeing, but being seen. And another, the man in a pale linen suit, the woman in a purple-and-yellow shot silk dress, at a café terrace table, she engrossed in a small book bound in red leather, he watching the world, smoking, an ankle on his knee, a hand on the ankle. Elegant was the only word.

"Who?" He had woken up that aristocrat girl of his, shaken her out of a dream and into the unforgiving light, and all for nothing. She stared at him irritably through her messy hair.

"The Armenians."

But the woman from the couple, it gradually became plain to Henri, was not Armenian, had no memories of cold deserts or burning water, but remembered forests with a shiver. She shared a vision of a train stopped in an open space alongside a bank of trees, and out of them rode not a solitary cyclist bringing bad news, but men on horseback, bringing fire and lead. Cossacks, Henri understood, imagining their big coats, fur hats, facial hair, fierce eyes, Nagant rifles, sabers, but perhaps it was the Red Army – they wore big coats, too. Big coats were the thing for Russia and the places caught in its orbit, weren't they...? The woman was no longer sure – it didn't matter who the men were; their mission was the same as the raping, pillaging hordes of old from the east, and it was destruction. She remembered not knowing anything for sure anymore, nor, most of the time, caring.

Her man was out in a café's vestibule area, holding their coats and chatting to a small group of acquaintances engaged in an endless round of leave-taking. In the company of nobody, it seemed, just Henri nearby in one of his contented hazes, the woman remembered Chisinau in flames. She was cursed, she claimed, with the vision of the synagogue on her street burning down. Henri looked up, saw her bow her head and tell somebody out of his view – a boy barman, he saw, stuck with the lowly job of sweeping up the last leavings of a crowd and indulging them in their woeful last-thing-at-night reminiscences – that she'd disdained and distrusted the synagogue's denizens. She had even spat, sometimes, like her father, at the sight of them. "But I never wished destruction on them," she said, her teeth bared. "Never."

The boy came into Henri's view, sweeping, and nodded without catching her eye, and said nothing. Henri said, "Where is Chisinau?" He had never heard of it. She half-turned. Her glance was poison. He smiled it away. She would tell him another time, he was certain.

Henri had neither sea nor deserts nor forests in his head to plague him, only cold school corridors and dinners, endless drives that ended as picnics with the rain beating on the car roof and dribbling down the windows, and scratchy jumpers and blankets. There were also the scolding silences of his parents, incoherent radio voices in the background, the dull words in the books he was made to read, and the intangible teenage wishes for stuff, for girls, for escape. This may possibly have been the metaphorical kind found in narcotics, even though he had never heard the word.

When Henri was thirteen, an uncle made a surprise Christmas visit, and presented him with a model war plane in molded plastic. Henri was a bit old for modelling. He didn't want a war plane at all, and certainly not so badly that he would waste his time pulling the parts off their plastic trellis and gluing the thing together. It sat in its box, disdained, unattended and forgotten, until one day, with nothing else to do, and his last library book finished, and the library closed, and a fear of going downstairs in case he was given some beastly task to do, it drew his attention. Henri was distracted by the fumes from the modelling glue. Instead of being distressed, he was intrigued, and then mesmerized in a way he couldn't remember later. The war plane remained unmade; Henri had forgotten it once more. In any case, he had used up all the glue, inhaled it in the form of those fumes, he was astonished to realize. He still didn't know the word narcotic. Over the years he bought enough modelling glue to make a fleet of war planes, a flotilla of battleships. He thought of that as his own metaphor for the so-called post-war period, with all those wars great powers kept thinking up to occupy them: leave the military hardware unbuilt – that was the thing – abandon the fighting, just inhale the fumes and turn on the light inside and look deep into the mind where the secrets lie, the essence of good at their core, expose them to the light.

He pondered those charged memories whenever he ran into the man from Armenia, or so he felt sure, and the woman from Chisinau, wherever that was, and was invited to share a cigarette or a glass of wine with them.

"The water is an open space," it was pointed out to them in those passing conversations – once by a Londoner at the end of his good looks and good luck, counting his last few francs on the coast. He was spending them on a coffee before killing his last hour in Nice with a walk to the airport, to be returned to the dull job that, he promised, was genuinely not worth talking about. He had once been in the Royal Navy, he said. They had all agreed about the danger in the water, suddenly silent, cautious, and glancing at one another, pondering the graveyard the water provided for many.

Henri had never thought about that as a kid. The Haven in Boston had not seemed dangerous, nor the Witham, nor the sea off Skegness, and Grimsby.

The Londoner had laughed a little, realized, "Anybody who lives by the sea must fear the water." He had dipped his head and laughed, at himself, and to himself, and said sorry – sorry. Nobody knew what for; he was English, and didn't need a reason, Henri explained later. If there had been an offence, the couple had forgiven him, and bought him a brandy to settle his nerves – and Henri too, whose nerves, dulled almost out of existence, needed no settling – before he trusted his homecoming to the open space above all that water.

The water's dangers were quick and obvious and merciful, Henri thought. He looked at the woman, and for a moment thought he'd merely imagined her story about being on the train at the mercy of men on horses. The forests and the deserts hid a different malevolence, he woke up thinking.

They told Henri that they were rewarded for their troubles with dreams in which they were forgiven for wishing harm. Henri was fascinated. People didn't talk about their dreams back in Boston. "Maybe they didn't have any," he joked to me. "People in Boston." And the people he knew the more he'd got into drugs, they were never sure of the dividing line between dreaming and waking. The couple's dreams, he learned, were marbled with the quality of a mercy denied to the people of their origins: members of their families, friends of long standing or only passing interest, local shopkeepers, the alien Jews in the synagogues of Chisinau. In their dreams, the mercy was even extended to the alien Turks and mountain bandits, the alien Cossacks and Red Armies and commissars, who'd in turn made them into aliens. In their dreams, Henri understood, lay history, the bitterness of their own stories weaving in and out of it, evading it and casting it off, only to find it waiting for them further up the line.

Three

"The Jews have a song about Chisinau," the woman said. Henri had forgotten how the conversation had turned to music. "It was their grave, and yet they sing about it." She sounded quietly outraged. "It would be like you," she prompted her man, "singing a song about Smyrna."

Smyrna rang some terrible bell in the back of Henri's mind. He wasn't sure why.

"There are plenty of songs about Smyrna." Henri's new companion laughed. He said he didn't particularly like them; they extolled its virtues, and left out its flaws, and that wasn't the genuine Smyrna.

"How does it go?" he asked the woman, to tease her. "The Jews' song about Chisinau?"

She expressed surprise at the question with her brows, waved it away as an irrelevance. She had forgotten Chisinau, she claimed. That got the man smiling.

"Chisinau?" As he had done in that late-night café, Henri said, "Where is that?"

"Bessarabia," the man said, and because Henry couldn't very well ask where again, he put on a knowledgeable face and nodded.

The woman was irritated, she told Henri – it had to be Henri, as he was probably the only one there who'd not heard her say this before – that anybody should remember its name, parceled out as it was among Russians and Ukrainians and Romanians and those who'd been dubbed Moldovans. Who knew anymore, and who cared? Henri saw, all the same, that the city was festering away in her head.

She sat on the balcony overlooking the dump, her feet up on the railing. As the dark came down, she watched a long-legged spider on the wall. It was at an unnatural angle, and some of its legs looked longer than others, crooked, doubly alien. She gave it a nudge with her foot. It twitched once, but refused to be intimidated. She raised her foot, and crushed the spider, flicked its remains away with her imperfect, painted toes.

She looked up, sensed rather than saw the junkie watching her from the doorway.

He said, "Thank you for your… kind hospitality." He could have sworn he'd seen the spider breathing. He had to fight the urge to say, he wasn't afraid of you, and you weren't afraid of him, so why did you do that? There was no way to say it without sounding critical of his host, this woman who had cooked him a rather… bland dinner, it was fair to say, but in good faith. She had also plied him over-generously with booze and listened politely to some rambling stories from his errant, fractured life on the Blue Coast. The most amusing part of the conversation for Henri had been the revelation that she had never heard of the Rolling Stones; she had looked blank and almost confused when the man had suggested that even cannibals in Papua New Guinea had heard of the band. "I'm on my way, now."

In need of a fix, he had to go. He had given in to the urge the week before, at their place. On his first visit, he had splashed some blood onto their bathroom floor. It was only a little, but he had managed to hide it by rubbing away the flaky plaster and leaving a scar he couldn't help but look at each time he was in there. Not cool.

She said, "I wanted to talk to you."

He was still m'sieu to her, and to him she was madame. He had overstayed his welcome after dinner, he was sure; he might have been young, and a junkie, a specter of the parts of the sixties that had refused to swing, but he was still English, after all, stuck with his parents' manners. He said, "Sure."

She said, "That stuff in your eyes."

There was no hiding from the words. Henri hung his head, not ashamed, exactly. He felt a part of himself chipped away, to know that he was quite so… transparent. He could no longer be m'sieu once she'd said that.

Perhaps she read his mind. She stated his name. She turned, smiled kindly, and said, "Can you be a darling, and get some for me?"

Four

The couple had gone under a variety of names that reminded them of different times in their lives – and different eras of the century behind them, Henri saw. In the still of the night and the light of the day, however, no matter what it said on their collection of identity cards, driving licenses, police records, or passports, the man was Armen, and the woman Luciana. Those were their final names, and they would never escape them; "The times are less... fluid, these days," Armen would say. Henri heard regret in his tone, as well as relief.

Henri was not the only visitor. There was Jules, a retired waiter, a friend who went way back to when they could all still be described as young. He had sometimes slipped them a drink on the house, and, when they were flush, accepted one from them. Not really a drinker, he had often poured it into a glass, then down the sink, or donated it to a decent colleague or a gamer down on his luck; the drink didn't matter, just the gesture of good faith, and the house being short of a measure at the accounting end of the day. He had winked at them, if it seemed safe, when he saw that they were setting up a game he understood but, paradoxically, couldn't see. Their trade relied on that, of course.

Jules hadn't cared that they fleeced the house; the house fleeced the world when it could. Jules' father had been an old communist, idealistic, kind, and deluded, of course, and imprisoned for his troubles, then shot by his own side in the Spanish Civil War. As far as Jules was concerned, the fat cats could take a hit – Armen's and Luciana's modest mastery with the cards made only imperceptible dents in the houses' coffers.

Henri often heard it said that everybody had a story, probably from Armen. It was this that had made him develop his own, I suppose, until every line of it incorporated parts of others' stories, like a sonnet turning into a novel. Soon, Jules' stories became subsumed into Henri's own, and would bug him, like all the stories he heard, and please him, he said, to his grave.

Jules saw a lot of eye-opening behavior in his time on the coast, but only one story really haunted him. One day when he was a young man, an apprentice to the hospitality trade at the Hotel Negresco, he'd got into the service elevator, and had been greeted by an older waiter with an excited gleam in his eye. Jules had learned to be wary of the older staff, especially if they gleamed or beamed; either they wanted more than a friendly word from him, or were snooty, jealous of his youth and disdainful of his inexperience, and had rehearsed some cruel witticism with which to make him feel less handsome and cocky – less young. On this occasion the older man had held a fat wallet out to Jules, who saw at once that it was stuffed with notes – there had to be thousands of francs there, a portable fortune. "Found it," the man had spluttered out. "In a toilet – imagine." Jules had imagined. He had eyed the wallet with hunger. He had looked down at his fingernails, traces of silver polish in them, his knuckles raw, his socks damp, the ends of his shirt tucked deep into his trousers to hide the flecks of mold on them, all from winter nights in his garret in the hotel. The paltriness of his wage made him brave, and the dank poverty to which his chosen career had brought him, and, without looking at the man, he'd suggested they split it, a modest seventy-thirty, a finder's fee for the bearer, and a don't-tell-anybody fee for Jules, the potential grass.

It was near Christmas. Jules had a Dickensian vision of himself riding an enormous goose to his parents' house. He would feed the entire village, would become a Holy Season legend of the Alpes-Maritimes.

The silence that descended on the elevator had more than a lack of speech to it. The man had been outraged; he was going to hand the wallet in, of course. This was genuinely the last thing Jules had thought of him doing. His own outrage, while silent, matched the other man's. "How dare you." The older waiter had puffed his little chest out, stood on his heels, said, "Why you… little… thief." At that, Jules had fixed him with a sneer, and had also fixed himself with a determination to tell as many people as possible that this… fool was going to hand the wallet back – a mere drop in some rich bastard's ocean of cash, one he'd barely notice once he'd dispatched the fool with a pat on the back and a sou for his trouble. Jules had been disgusted, and had exited the lift with a haughty gait, and a renewed sense of the flaws in human nature.

Jules had moved on from the Negresco – as had the fool – but years on, Jules occasionally saw him in the street, old now, still poor, but still self-righteous, presumably. Every time he did, Jules wanted to cross the street and kick him. No matter how much money had passed through Jules' hands in the intervening time, that little thirty percent of a lost fortune ching-chinged through his dreams and daydreams. Each time he heard it, he would be prompted to ponder missing his chance of legendary status back in his youth when he was cold, and damp, poor, and miserable, put-upon, and patronized. Armen enjoyed the story, in a semi-sadistic way, but his sympathy for the young Jules was such that he felt some of the pain, so there was also something of the masochist in him when he egged Jules on to retell it for each new acquaintance. They would all laugh, and shake their heads, and Jules' hand, ruefully.

Armen was a fatalist about money, Henri understood, but also an optimist and, in a way, a fantasist. When it came, it came; when it was gone, you went and got some more. It… explained him, a little, Henri thought.

There were other old hotel and casino staff who dropped in, people who had lived among others all their lives, and served them, squeezing nimbly between elbows, and tables, and a million fragments of conversation, and thought they'd grab a bit of space in their retirements. Many of them had moved out of Nice into the hinterland around Vence and St. Paul, but had then missed the crush and Babel of people, their vexations and frustrations, joys and miseries, and had moved back to the coast.

To add a glimmer of youth, there was a cast of young students from several dance academies, where both Armen and Luciana had taught from time-to-time, the carefree swing of Latin American and the rigid gothic seriousness of the tango. The students brought wine and pastis and established a party atmosphere. They were charming to their hosts and their older friends almost without noticing them, and partied in between them. They broke out of their obsession with one another to smile, and express crazy delight at something Armen had said, or to admire Luciana's favorite yellow dress or her earrings that had once belonged to a 'certain lady in Monaco'.

Neighbors looked in, and discussed the weather, the traffic, the tourists, the disgraceful times they were living in, sometimes, the equally shocking prices of things. They remarked on the view when the sun hid the dump with its glare, and, in the summer, cooked some of the mysterious, vile substances down there, sent up in the occasional puff of acrid steam. None of the visitors outstayed their welcome, except Henri, sometimes, and they left the apartment to regain its silence until the morning broke it.

The neighbors remarked on the junkie, Henri could tell, but not when he was there; the old woman Henri understood to be Greek, the bland man with the Polish name, around Henri's age, getting pear-shaped fat, who blinked owlishly behind his glasses, and the young woman Henri mistook for a waitress, who was a hairdresser. He smiled at them all the same, and accepted the mixture of curiosity and censure they both brought and took with them.

Five

Luciana didn't appreciate the silence as much as Armen. During the day there was rarely complete silence, with the grind of drills from the repair shop downstairs, the banging of resistant panels, and, the couple thought, the hiss of the respraying of getaway cars so that they could be used again when the banks had refilled their vaults. There was also a radio emitting tinny music, drowned out by discussions of sport, pop, and politics as the mechanics snatched a break in the sunshine – where Paris St. Germain merged with Raymond Poulidor, Johnny Halliday with Francoise Hardy, de Gaulle with Pompidou, and Algeria with Tunisia. Luciana complained about all these sounds to Henri, but with a touch of good humor, so he assumed they suited the background of her moods.

Once the shop closed, the silence descended, and Luciana sat on the balcony, fanning herself, and looked up startled at the merest noise. She heard stray shouts from boys playing football on the street side, and the occasional thud of a ball. A water hammer in one of the nearby blocks always began sometime before she really noticed it, like tinnitus, perhaps triggered by somebody along the street taking a shower; the plumbing was connected haphazardly, as if landlords and workmen had decided to save on costs, split the difference and leave a mystery behind in the pipes to vex generations of tenants.

She thought about the water, looked over the dump to the sea, remembered Bessarabia, landlocked, and safe, until it was no longer safe to be anywhere. She remembered sitting on a ship in the Polish port of Gdynia, on the cold edge of Europe, among people who feared the slightest noise, the slightest sight of a man wearing an armband, carrying a club, carelessly giving out bad food – the smell of them after a month without a change of clothes. There were silences broken by the cry of a child, or even sometimes a song, a laugh, the mention of Walt Disney; absurd, to laugh in such a place, to sing. She was no longer sure whether she had really looked out a porthole into the darkness, imagining America, whether she had indeed remarked to a hope-haunted woman nearby, "We'll never see Mickey Mouse. I can feel it. I feel nothing else in this terrible place, but I feel that."

Armen counted it as a failure, he told Henri, that he had never quite been able to prise Luciana completely away from the fields of Bessarabia; there was still a part of her hiding in a barn, behind a hedgerow, or a stack of hay, the city on fire, sparks on the wind, the fear of conflagration in those fields the Jews sang about. He had sought out the Klezmorims' song, of course, thought it unremarkable, at first, a novelty, and then found it generous, forgiving, a tribute to an alien land that had, for all its faults, and those of its people, become home. He could not think of one song about the Blue Coast. Its successful people were too busy to write songs – he supposed the Rolling Stones were a necessary exception, but they weren't serenading the Bay of Angels, but the backwoods of the United States – and its losers were too bitter to sing.

Six

Luciana had taken up the habit of the occasional slamming of doors when she went in and out. It was a surrender, people supposed, to some urge deep inside her to seek the harmless violence, hear the impact, the echo through the silence.

The noise made Armen start, and cringe. The noisy percussion of door and frame reminded him of the prison in Smyrna before the War of Independence. It also brought him back to a miserable rice factory in which he worked in San Saba in Istria between the world wars – a place destined to be the site of mass murder – and of the heavy doors on the passenger boat on a stormy trip across the Adriatic when the sea toyed with anything that dared to float on it, everybody in and out all night onto the deck to be sick off the side.

It came out once during an argument, and then in the murmured aftermath, that Luciana had grown up in silence in Chisinau, in a squeaking-clean respectable townhouse appropriate to thriving merchants like her father. She heard her mother drop a pin there once, she swore. Two elder children had been miscarried, and then three younger ones, the same fate, not just gone, but never having appeared. They were still her siblings, though, making her an only child among ghosts. She had been able to bear the noises of the war, but the silences in between had brought voices that never quite addressed her, hands that never quite touched her, dolls and party dresses never quite loaned or hidden or ruined or given back.

Luciana told Henri the bare bones of these stories, perhaps because he seemed like a man who also didn't like silence – she was right – but probably just because he was there. Others saw only a junkie, dishonest, opportunistic, to be pitied or feared; Luciana's confidences were a sign that she trusted him, they both supposed.

"I threw my wedding ring out there." She nodded into the darkness over the dump. "One time we argued about my slamming the doors. It was a foolish... gesture. You are a young man," she pointed out. "You will make many foolish gestures." She nudged him, and almost laughed, and said, "But my advice is... don't."

Henri laughed, and protested, "Nothing wrong with foolish gestures." His whole life often felt like one. He recounted that, just that morning, he had picked up the phone at home to hear the voice of his countess' father. There had at one time been a regular... rigmarole, members of her family feigning Gallic surprise that a stranger should be answering the phone, pretending wrong numbers, saying nothing, even, vanishing with a click or slam. Henri's insistence on simply picking it up when it rang again had put the kybosh on that. That morning the father had asked, with his usual distaste, to speak to his daughter. Henri had never met him, nor ever would, he knew by then. He called him the archduke, for his own amusement – the countess had either not got the obvious joke, or disapproved of it – but that morning Henri had broken the joke out into the open, said, "At once, your highness," just to annoy him. "The little man striking back," he recalled for Luciana. "A little victory. A little... Guillotine, just taking off the end of his aristocratic fingernail for him. Did you get it back?"

"What?"

"The ring."

"The ring?" Luciana made a brief, ladylike snort. "Of course not. Once a thing is out there, it's lost forever."

"What did Armen do?"

"Do?" Luciana looked puzzled. "What was there to do?"

"Did he forgive you?" Henri knew the answer, was just making the conversation of a devil's advocate.

"Of course he did. I couldn't live with a man who didn't forgive." She thought about something, said, "Armen forgave the burning of his city."

"True." Henri had only vaguely heard of Smyrna before he met Armen.

"He forgave the genocide of his people."

"Genocide?" Henri considered the word in some discomfort. He thought of those persecutors and oppressors, from the highest-born to the lowest of the low, driving Armen's clever people into deserts, and into seas lit brightly with flames. He confessed later to the countess – and it was a failing, for sure, he knew – that he only wanted to discuss genocide with people who had seen it in old newsreels, not with people who had lived through it; that just wasn't right: what were you expected to say? To Luciana, he said something lame about a wedding ring being an important… thing.

She said, "After genocide, no… thing is important, no… trinket."

"Marriage is a convenience," Armen said from behind them. He came into the room, shutting the door gently. He passed Henri, patted him on a shoulder, and went and stood by Luciana. "It's a passport, a way to get a name on an identity card, or on a license to drive. The killing of women and children by great powers, sanctioned by other great powers, and by influential men who own newspapers, makes a lie out of the claim that marriage is some kind of sacred or social duty."

Henri looked down, dejected. The couple made noises of concern. Luciana's now, now was almost laughed out.

"Don't make foolish gestures." Armen held up his hand, and showed his own wedding ring. He grinned, said, "Or, if you do, make sure you are with somebody who doesn't, so that at least one of you has a ring left to pawn."

Seven

Before they had ever thought of rings, there had been a sweltering day not long after the World War, and a nondescript hotel dining room in a backstreet in Cannes. Henri understood that Armen had seen a young woman picking daintily, and a little fearfully, it seemed to him, at a mountain of food.

Her skin was white, almost, and Armen could see her most prominent veins through it. She had those enormous dark eyes – Balkan, he had already guessed – and her hair cut so short he could see the skin beneath it, for women a look familiar from Pathé News, of survivors from the privations of the World War.

He had engineered a conversation. She had ordered an espresso, she told him quietly but urgently, looking fearfully over his shoulder at the waiter. It was all she could afford, so she didn't understand the reason for having been brought plates bearing seafood, chicken, beef, pork, vegetables, and wilting salad. The waiter had just grinned when she tried to wave it all away. The telling thing for Armen, though, was that she was hungry, and would therefore eat, and would think about resolving the mystery later. Spontaneity was a quality he admired.

Armen had translated the waiter's cheerful remark that they had better enjoy it while it lasted; an electrical power failure had deactivated all the refrigerators on the entire block, so all the food had to go. Not since the Nazis had mobilized to occupy Vichy France had restauranteurs cleared their stock with such abandon. Once the electricity was back, and the patrons really did chip in to buy the generator they were forever procrastinating and bickering about, it was never going to happen again.

"But I can't eat all this," she'd protested.

"Nor me." He'd looked hard at her. He saw that she'd forgotten the worst of the war, when you'd eat anything put in front of you. He approved. He said. "They'll give it to some lucky dogs, no doubt."

But the dogs carried on with their dog lives. They remained starved in the streets and died from the impact of teeth or rocks or cars, or were imprisoned, flattened against the scented bosoms of bourgeoise women, died in stir-crazy dissipation. Armen and Luciana would be the ones with the luck.

He had almost mistaken her for a waif, struggling, and pathetic, but saw something stronger in her. Almost at once, he saw that such a mistake would be made by men to their disadvantage and, occasionally, ruin.

Armen pictured for Henri the people they'd chanced upon one night not long after that first meeting, an invitation to a card game from a tourist couple. The man, it soon became clear, had mistaken Armen for an occasional Blue Coast acquaintance. He had nudged him a few times, saying, "I like the new… wife. She's an improvement, huh?" He'd winked. "Huh?" Armen had nodded, twitched out the foolish smile expected of him, and had allowed himself to be persuaded into the game, Luciana watching.

She had soon understood that the player, an oilman who brought Texas around the world with him like an extra suitcase, talked too much to be any good at the games. His wife, aware of this, had sporadically reminded him, gently, to watch his hand. Because he was the kind of man who thought women knew nothing worth knowing, he had ignored her advice. She had pouted, widened her eyes at Luciana, as if to say there was much more where the money came from, and that she would be out shopping the next day anyhow, and hiring a maid, would be out on boat excursions, then drinking cocktails by the pool, and who was she to worry…

"Such men play to lose," Armen explained to Luciana early the next morning on the promenade, his bow-tie undone, his hand resting idly on a pocket full of cash. "They get a… thrill from losing, a strange kind of…

redemption. Who knows why? They don't know it, of course, and would deny it if you told them – it's all under the surface." The words prompted a thought of Smyrna, of chaotic wet glimpses of the disappearing city. "One hears of these men. We were lucky to have found him."

"I brought you the luck," she said.

He answered, "Of course you did. I will be lucky if you are with me, always."

They knew it wasn't just luck. Luciana had a gift for spotting the mugs, and Armen had sometimes demanded to know where it came from, and how on Earth she did it. "I have to keep some secrets," she'd improvised. It didn't matter; Armen didn't really want to know. "Because sometimes it's better to have a mystery than to solve one," she pointed out.

He wasn't sure if he agreed with that, but committed the few words to memory anyway.

They sought out more men like that first one. There was a look the losers had, they learned. They tended to go for the ones with women who accompanied them to the tables only to drink the indifferent champagne, excused themselves early and, bored, went to the bar, or for a massage, or a manicure, or walked out, sometimes, onto the Promenade des Anglais to seek an improvement in their fortunes in the form of a man with a better grip on his currency.

Those men who watched Luciana across gaming tables when their whole attention should have been on their play thought of her as beautiful, in some flawed way. She spoke softly, hesitantly, as if thinking about every word, the impression she wanted to make. Even her throwaway expressions, her dismissals – of films and their stars, of newspaper gossip, of the writers and intellectuals and politicians she dismissed as crooks and liars to the last man – seemed mannered, rehearsed, considered at great length for their nuance, and the impact they would make on listeners, but that was just her way.

She was able to be impassive, or to exude charm and make people feel at ease. Armen had long sought such a companion for the casino tables.

Together with this enigma of a woman, Armen made their ephemeral fortunes each night from bored adventurers going to seed, black marketeers, ex-Wehrmacht officers, ex-Ottoman functionaries who had served the last Sultan, long exiled from the republic the Turks had built over that dead empire. The first of them had been a court eunuch, a pale, thin ghost of a man, a fiercely competitive player who nevertheless showed too much to Luciana, playing her part to reduce him to a man who owned only what he stood up in. There were the civil servants a little too full of themselves, the moody, distracted spymasters, the bored magnates, the inept sheiks who thought they knew it all because they were rich and nobody ever dared to disagree with them, the aristocrats making forays into the world with their rare liquid assets before retiring hurt to their crumbling real estate, and one man who'd literally made his money for the Nazis' repugnant S.S., forging Bank of England notes to disrupt the British war effort. He came to Nice to lose his share of it, to start anew, an odd triumph in his eyes as he swept his chips over to Armen and Luciana, and tossed his last one to the drinks boy with a gesture that spoke of freedom at long last.

The millionaires were beyond the couple's reach, but they made their money from those who, like them, aspired. They lost it to them, too. "Maybe I've used up my magic," Luciana would suggest during a run of ill-luck, daring Armen to nod. He was never tempted. Luck was a specious, complex affair.

"Remember, I waited for you all my life," he told her, often. "Luck is not enough."

"What did you do without me?" She held a hand up to defend herself against some banal truth, some dismissal laughed out, but at other times would say, "No, really – what did you do? What were you?" And she imagined him at the tables without her, defenseless, see-through, a man of glass who looked like one of those Armenians she'd heard about in her youth, never to be trusted.

When she asked about his past, he didn't tell her at once about the work on boats and ships, the fishing, the dock work, the building jobs, the factory lines, the waiting, the commis-cheffing – making a thousand canapés, all exactly the same, every day for a year – the driving. "I came here and immediately became a flâneur," he told her. "A boulevardier. Of course." Armen's real story took years to tell. Luciana was both enthralled by each glimpse of it, and irritated by the gap it had revealed before it was filled in.

Who else knew his story, she wanted to know. "I've disappeared into history," he teased. "Like those Young Turk pashas wanted." When she got angry he promised her, "Nobody. I know nobody. Nobody knows me."

That wasn't true, of course, but all the same there was no real community of gamers. To outsiders, there may have been the impression of one. Armen and Luciana would find themselves nodding, imperceptibly, at least, to those they had been seeing at neighboring tables for years. Another year might go by, and they might smile, if all conditions were right – the subtle invitation in an expression, the cast of an eye, the way hands were spread out, and not, say, crossed defensively, fingers entwined, knuckles white. The people they recognized as such were, like them, pale in complexion, verging on grey, people who often only saw the sun as it rose, when they left the tables, and came out onto a terrace to take stock, pat their pockets and take a breath of the rarefied blue air.

Years went by, and they discussed the ups and downs of what passed for the community, the witchcraft that governed the tables, new faces in town, the appearance of a new prince among players, in a new car, new clothes – new shoes, wonderful shoes, that shone, and stood out a mile – a new apartment, new money with a snap to it. Then they noted his later appearance in a rooming house, those same clothes rank and tattered – and those awful shoes, their toes looking like animals' noses – the car gone, and his wry smile as he admitted, "It wasn't a great car, anyway." They glimpsed them occasionally as they walked in town or the suburbs, these once and future kings, their uncrowned heads down, carrying bread, cheese, saw them in the shops, exchanging mundane greetings with the shopkeepers that, for no apparent reason, sometimes became ordeals and inquisitions, a sea of memories too full of debris to swim through.

Eight

One of Armen's habits, by the time Henri knew him, was to walk down to the seafront in the early evening, and then the few kilometers along the coast to the Promenade des Anglais. He was often accompanied by Luciana, but if she wasn't up to the walk for any reason she took a bus and met him later. It both amused them and sparked a touch of regret whenever they paused for a drink in one of the bars near the casinos, and noted the patrons going in and coming out. Armen and Luciana had long been persona non grata at them all. That didn't stop the doormen from giving them a nod, friendly sometimes, knowing at others, and at other times censorious, as if it were an enormous cheek that they dared to show their faces, even in passing.

None of those doormen Henri saw, whenever he observed this tableau, or became part of it, had been the gatekeepers at the casinos when Armen and Luciana were making their fleeting fortunes. Those top-hatted window dummies had a rogues' gallery memorized, Luciana and Armen among them, and only a vague and hearsay notion of their transgressions – despite their sworn role never to let the pair darken the casinos' august doors – which were nothing compared to those of the shysters and sharpers the casinos were up against by the end of the sixties.

Henri's nights were riven with sleeplessness, and with heroin, its pleasing, driving glow spiking inside him, then its long, gentle diminution. He walked the promenade alone if he didn't run into Armen and Luciana, and frequented the bars tucked away behind it. He had got talking to one or two of the doormen – never the croupiers, semi-officially forbidden such places – late at night. They were easy enough to spot, their hats concertinaed or stowed in boxes, their collars removed, collar studs gleaming, defenses down, and ready to talk frankly after an evening of fakery in their greetings or the tough talk they had to adopt, sometimes, in their rebuttals. Ready for some wine, too, Henri saw, and, when he was flush, obliged. Cagey, Henri thought, as they spotted the opiates in his eyes, wary, perhaps, at first, but they didn't judge; they remained discreet, even off-duty.

The doormen may have looked like amicable robots, but they had ears and eyes and memories, and had their stories, like anybody else, and the urge to tell them. Henri got them in dribs and drabs, the placing of fingers spread in a palm or a twitch of the lips implying answers to the questions he learned to infer.

He both enjoyed and was shocked at the tale that featured a foolish senior British civil servant losing, on the turn of a card, his London flat to Armen and Luciana – "A tiny apartment," the doorman thought. He made a classic French face for Henri, brows elevated, lips puffed out momentarily. He was impressed, briefly, then no longer. "The turn of a card, m'sieu," he reminded Henri. "And – pouf! – everything gone, like a magic show."

Henri remembered Armen and Luciana dismissing London, or so the gist told him. He hadn't been listening with all his attention, caught as he was in his first conversation with the couple's young hairdresser neighbor. He had wondered what had taken them to London. They were lamenting that their visit had stranded them far from the Swinging London they'd been expecting. The streets had been full of loud boys sporting blue-and-white scarves – match day somewhere, Henri had guessed, which could be an alarming spectacle. "The drunks," Luciana said. "How can anybody be that drunk?" The drunks filled a park overlooked by elegant Victorian tenements, fought among themselves without... decorum, Henri heard, and laughed, wondered how anybody could fight with decorum, unless they were Muhammad Ali.

"A horror," Luciana had swiped the memory away with a hand. Henri had nodded along in his own conversation, but watched Luciana smile self-effacingly as if she could look into his mind, hear his thoughts: genocide was a horror, he was thinking, and the men in coats coming out of the trees, the Cossacks or the Red Army, and Chisinau in flames, and the fate of the people in the synagogue… and Smyrna, the fire and the water. Those were horrors. London was just full of snooty wage slaves, and old-school drunks, and deluded hippies, and mouthy kids, like anywhere, and yes, like anywhere else, well-fed hooligans in sheepskin coats and scarves.

"These terrible, terrible – pubs." Luciana laughed the word out in English, made it not terrible, but comic. "They drink and drink." She made the height of a very large pint glass with her hands. "But it doesn't make them happy."

Armen had mentioned the rowdy children with wet hair and socks that wouldn't stay up, the shops full of cheap, and bad, food, the awful cafés, the markets, urging Luciana to repeat the mantra she'd memorized: four-fuh-five-shillins-yer-tea-towels. It was a passable impression, and made them both burst into laughter. Henri had meant to ask them more about their sojourn in run-down London, but it was a place he neither knew nor cared for, and he was happy to be sidetracked by his friends' neighbor.

The story had made more sense once he'd heard about their winning an entire flat from some poor bankrupt bastard. He had seen them in a new light for a minute, and it wasn't a flattering one.

Years later, stood on a winter corner near St. Giles Hospital, experiencing the first sweats of his thousandth withdrawal, he was for a moment unable to believe he'd ever lived that other life on the boulevards of Nice and the backstreets up the hill to the Arab quarter. His memories of a Blue Coast countess, and shooting up the best heroin in the world in the basement of a mansion with multi-millionaire rock stars and their friends, must have seemed like a vivid mirage.

Along with another of the doormen, Henri tutted over the unfortunate luck of an Italian Conte who'd spent an ill-advised evening with the couple. He had been an arts patron and collector, too charming and benign to be a skilled gamer. Courtesy of the Conte, Armen and Luciana had a small, eerie townscape by Italian surrealist Giorgio de Chirico on their wall for many years, until it disappeared in sketchy but, probably, uncomplicated circumstances. "Shot himself in the English cemetery in Rome," the doorman remembered. "Not because of this incident," he assured Henri. "It was years later, over a woman, or a man. He was too benign to fall in love, as well, it seemed." Henri marveled not at the story, but at the sorrow it brought out from within him, the idea of such a man in this day and age of brash informality.

Years later, and again on a Camberwell corner, he added the Conte's story to his own as he felt the first cluck of cold turkey. In his head it was accompanied by a tune his parents had played on their gramophone, about a little bird who died of love, singing, somewhat absurdly, willow, tit willow, tit willow. It brought back those parents to whom he'd not given a thought in years. It brought Henri to me, off night shift at St. Giles, me grey in the face and he yellow in his – jaundice, I diagnosed off the cuff – and both of us craving breakfast. It brought him back to St. Giles that afternoon, dying not of love but of something more easily treatable, to his favorite bed overlooking the grounds. His return was spoiled only by the bloke in the next bed, an old man who spoke to himself in Polish and Yiddish and moaned while awake and asleep. Mr. Reyman was quietened only by a cup of tea, and then, alarmingly, and finally, by an enormous hemorrhage that spilled out of his mouth and all over his bedclothes, nobody near enough to close the curtains on him in time.

It wasn't a doorman, but Jules, the old waiter, who told Henri about Armen's historical revenge on a bodyguarded Turkish businessman known along the coast as the Saracen. The man had noted Armen's look, one still seen in Istanbul as well as the Turkish lands approaching both the Black Sea border with Georgia and the Caucuses mountains, and had been careful of him as a man wronged by those not-so-young Turks. But perhaps not careful enough.

Armen's claim to have forgiven the genocide of his people may or may not have been true, but his habitual cordiality was offered to anybody he met, pasha or pleb. "It was one of Armen's secrets," Jules confided to Henri. "All players are cordial, of course, for it can be no other way. But his politeness was... disarming, you understand? Most... literally disarming. I can't explain it any other way. And it worked its magic gradually, like a..." He had already pointed a finger towards Henri, going to say narcotic, Henri supposed. "Anesthetic," he said at last.

When Armen was done with the Saracen, his final hand of cards revealed devastation, it had been related to Jules, an explosive resolution to a long bout of doubling, the multiples of which only the croupier was keeping a record, discreetly noting them on a pad, which allowed for the coup to be as enormous as the onlookers wanted it to be when they related it later. The final hand had got even some of the most jaded of them gasping, their eyes drawn back and forth in fascination to the pile of rectangular plaques mid-table that meant serious money. The Saracen had just bowed his enormous head and watched the dealer paddle those plaques away from him across the table and, slowly, had reached out and shaken Armen's hand, murmuring that it had been a pleasure.

"I'm a man who appreciates a fortune," Jules reminded Henri, who remembered Jules' sad story of his long-lost loot in the Negresco. He knew that all the tales had their own deep truths about chance, and marked the fine differences that led to much or nothing. As he always did, he let Jules' tale, and those of the doormen, revive his own story with a drop of color; that story of his, it sometimes seemed, was often on the point of receding into a fog of black and white and grey, great colors for Camberwell.

Nine

It amused Armen that he and Luciana were probably as memorable to Nice people around the promenade as the merchants in his boyhood Smyrna had been to him, tramping their routes from Basmahane station down the so-called 'grands rues'. That was his first French, he remembered, the international language adopted by the traders. It had been handed down somewhat inexpertly by the diplomats, he remembered, though the rumor surfaced occasionally that they were neglecting it in the pursuit of perfecting their Turkish.

He remembered the trader who hired a man to drive a donkey when he was in funds, and who drove the beast himself when he wasn't, then carried his goods on his back when he couldn't even afford to hire a donkey, and put up with the laughter. Armen joined in with it, but one day was moved to help the man, waving away the promise of eventual recompense. There was also the kindly head of the trade office, and his less kind chief clerk, who scattered beggars with a thick walking stick. Armen would never forget the giant policeman who bore livid claw marks on his face from fighting a wolf on the slopes of Mount Ararat, nor the woman whose scarf sometimes slipped to show the hole under her ear from a bandit's gunshot in the wilds of Western Armenia – the place the Turks called Eastern Anatolia. They had all fled from there at one time or another, sensing the threat from pious Ottomans and godless communists, and had been drawn to cosmopolitan Smyrna, and its position of safety, protection by interested European powers, and escape, on the Aegean Sea.

On the Promenade des Anglais, Armen had for years noted recognition in the greetings he received. The minutely bowed heads, barely-seen waves, neutral glances from the odd policeman – those never changed – the winks or sneers from the casino doormen, all reminded him of the details hidden in the everyday bustle of Haynots, Smyrna's Armenian quarter.

On the front in Nice, Armen joked that promenading was the only way an elegant pair could walk. He sported neat suits, while Luciana wore her couture dresses – getting threadbare, but, in an increasingly casual age, retaining an air of class that still showed among the nylon shirts, polyester sports coats and denim jeans that had almost overnight become everyday wear. He and Luciana joined a procession of the ages along the promenade, of people whose lives were written into it, who could now remember no other life. They moved comfortably in between those who stayed a week, and just appeared, sometimes, as if they were a part of the place. Then they were whisked away by train or plane, jolted back into a life that didn't include the promenade, the Negresco, the sight of Armen and Luciana, the slow-moving herds of people who belonged there.

"People like us," Armen had given the picture of himself and Luciana as Blue Coast fixtures in a half-hearted, half-thought-out way, almost talking to himself as he drank a breakfast coffee with Henri. He looked at Henri's scrappy cheesecloth shirt, his scruffy jeans, the start of a hole in one knee, for Heaven's sake, poor chap. Henri's ruinous sandals were like the one Armen had once seen in a history museum; it had belonged to a Roman soldier, and had survived the centuries, but only just. Then he thought of his own right shoe; classy black hand-tooled leather, it looked the part, nobody could deny, but its shameful secret was a cardboard plug to keep out the rain for another season. "And like you too, Henri, of course."

"Me?"

"You belong here, now."

"Really?"

Until he got to Nice, Henri had never thought of himself as belonging anywhere. He'd never belonged in Boston, nor at his dreadful prep and public schools, nor at Durham University, where he'd lasted a year. Bereft of a more original idea, he had headed down to Swinging London. He hadn't belonged there, either, for sure, among those hippies, kidding themselves that they were changing the world with their Jesus hair and their beards that hid their features, their LSD and loon pants – fakes, all of them.

He had met the countess in London. He heard her complaining about those same hippies, and about the crowds in Harrods, and the traffic, and a host of other things; bobbies on bicycles two-by-two were all very well, but they were useless if they couldn't speak at least a little French to guide her in such a heaving metropolis. Henri had never been to Harrods, nor had he noticed the traffic, really. He had always affected a natural avoidance of policemen on any form of transport. His sudden display of an utterance or two recalled from his school French had enchanted the countess, while her seemingly endless supply of heroin had worked a similar magic on him. It was enough to take them south together for the winter: Nice, of course, where Henri resumed the language that had plagued him at school, and found a new facility with it, in a place where he felt he could fit in, at last.

In the countess's pad in St. Paul, though, he was made to skulk, at first, when any of the relatives made a state visit, and then to vacate it, just temporarily, when she confessed that she had told her mother he was a workman. He said he understood, and didn't care. He did

– of course he did. Any moments of indignation he conjured up were soon subsumed into the thought that eventually tagged onto them: he was a junkie and, as such, didn't belong anywhere, and had no right to feel slighted, or disdained. Even at Keith Richards' place, where he was a junkie among other junkies, he was still, when the day dawned and he came down, nauseous when hungry, nauseous after eating, hating the bright light, hating the darkness, just a junkie.

He was stung, all over again, indignant, again, outraged. He gave in to it all and raged, just once, ran out into a storm, dodged the cars, blocked his ears from their devils' horns, his ranting and cursing rousing a nearby millionaire or two. He was eased in off the road by Bill Wyman's driver, a kind man who saw the catharsis in Henri's act and linked Henri's arm firmly in his own and, in that Mediterranean rain, kindly in its own way, danced him back to the house like in a choreograph from Singin' in the Rain. He bade him sit in a stately cane armchair, and told him a joke, made him laugh, made him toast, urged him to eat it, and to wash it down with a bowl of milky coffee, like any other denizen of the coast.

Ten

Camberwell in autumn prompted Henri into recalling for me that there was a kind of ennui particular to the Blue Coast in autumn and winter, or so local intellectuals were fond of saying. I couldn't imagine the mood of the colder months on the Riviera being worse than the scene we looked out on from Nick's café: rain-swept trees, muddy pavements, people laboring along on their way to the new magistrate's court in teeth-gritted determination. We avoided going out into it while staring into our tepid grey tea, with Jimmy Young blathering inanely on Radio Two in the background, oblivious to history and the pressure in the air, the moisture in the clouds, the deadliness of water. Henri's Blue Coast gloom came from his own day-to-day trials, but he said it wasn't all in the collective mind, and he often sensed something strange in the air in the few weeks before autumn came, as if the residents couldn't bear thinking about the time that must follow. The well-heeled, such as Henri's countess, never spoke of it. Their awareness of it was only noticeable when they snapped at one another, and complained about the miserable service from the working people, the reluctant help, the half-hearted acceptance of skivvy jobs, and even of tips deemed to be too light.

Henri suspected it was peculiar only to those who felt let down by the Blue Coast, who'd made their way there when younger and full of vitality and ambition, only to find that the coast, and its people, had disappointed them, season after season. And here was another at its end, with just a little less hope for the next.

He included himself among the disappointed – it was for better and for worse if you belonged to the Blue Coast, and it seemed that Armen was right, and he did indeed belong there. In truth, Henri passed many days harboring little hope of anything other than getting through them; he had no major disappointments, he realized, because he'd never worked up any major expectations. If this made him melancholy, nobody else knew, except, perhaps, Armen, who had seen so much of it in his days, and didn't need to look too closely at Henri to work it out. Those late-night doormen and one-time waiters, the young dancers from the academies, and Armen's and Luciana's neighbors, Blue Coast denizens, and Blue Coast interlopers, they all greeted Henri with a kind of muted, long-suffering cheer, and expected something similar back, an impossible mixture of honesty and diplomacy. By the time I met Henri, he was claiming melancholy as a cloud particular to Camberwell. He looked up and laughed with a caught-out expression when I suggested it was he who'd brought it from the bright and glowing South of France to murky old South London.

Luciana sometimes noted his mood if her mind was clear of her own preoccupations. She welcomed him in with the words, "No countess tonight?" only in an effort to induce a little gossip out of him; she'd resigned herself to her curiosity about Henri's companion remaining unsatisfied. Included in her welcome was a warm smile, and cheeks offered for the barest of kisses. He usually joined in with a murmur of regret, knowing it was just conversation. His countess was never going to accompany him to his friends' place, was only ever going to slum it with the likes of the Stones and their other hangers-on. In any case, she was often absent, out on the sometimes complicated business of scoring, and, her allowance gone on heroin and Henri, of blagging money from various relatives; a night out here, a day out there, an overnight stay, unpalatable meals with pickled relatives that went on all evening, a visit to a dreary concert, the opening of an art exhibition or a play.

Luciana was amused by Henri's occasional report that the countess would wake up once in a while obsessed manically with getting the apartment cleaned. He thought it had to do with surprise parental visits. Nothing else would matter until she tracked down some local crone who would overcharge her, the whole saga ending in a sulk followed by a big row. Luciana believed Henri when he said the countess genuinely didn't know how to clean an apartment. "She never had to learn," Luciana murmured. "She is primarily a lady, of course." Henri would suppose so, as neutrally as he could; his first thought was nearly always that the countess was primarily a junkie, just like him. He had to confess that he also didn't know how to clean an apartment – especially one full of Empire furniture, rare tapestries that attracted the dust, hideous knick-knacks that had, pointlessly, survived several revolutions and two world wars, dull paintings and leather-bound books that were priceless, and somehow yet spectacularly useless. The times being what they were, he was never expected even to try.

Henri liked visiting Luciana's and Armen's apartment because it had the qualities of home, he realized, in some scattered dream of home: it was a place in which he was welcomed with smiles; he wasn't expected to be quiet, nor to be amusing, nor to be elsewhere. It also had wooden furnishings that were neither modern nor classic, could be lounged-on, scuffed, marked by accident, and no undue fuss made, books with sun-faded covers and edges, which he was invited to read and keep, bring back or pass on, as it pleased him, and an old radio he was allowed to tune to the local pop stations. He liked the big windows and their yellow curtains, Luciana's favorite color, and the space of pure, shimmering light they framed out the back. There was also that view of the sea, glittering, truly blue, sometimes, right enough, or shrouded in mist, a smear made by a child's finger. Henri understood that he should ignore the dump, and pretend it wasn't there, look instead beyond, to the sea, and the sky, dotted by the yellow planes that roamed the coast in search of wind and weather patterns, and fire, of shipping veering off course, of smugglers on their cautious way to and fro by sea or land.

"I love the little planes," Luciana sometimes told guests.

If they felt at ease with her, they laughed, and said, "The coast guards? But why?"

"Because they're yellow," she said. "Of course. Who can't love yellow?" Or sometimes she said, "They guard the coast. They make me feel safe."

"Really?" The question often came disguised as a laugh. "But they miss so much. Only last week, a consignment of cocaine got through to Spain."

"No." Somebody mentioned the semi-legendary French Connection. "Heroin."

"Heroin, then."

"Look." Henri twitched at the repeated words, changed the subject in search of a rest from them, perhaps. "They're doing a loop-the-loop." He adopted that child's finger to illustrate the child's phrase, and pointed excitedly. He was allowed to do that at Armen's and Luciana's, too, be excited, and not grave.

And a girl drowned, Luciana remembered, she told Henri later, a pale young rich thing who dived off her own boat in her red bikini and, unnoticed by the two-man crew, got caught by a cramp, a change in the weather or the visibility – didn't get through to anywhere but the other side. The planes missed her, too.

"They find what they find," Luciana was able to say with a laugh.

Henri saw what she meant; the planes had a reassuring permanence. It didn't matter what they found, as long as they were seen to be up there.

"Planes are not the same in peacetime," Armen said to a guest, an earnest girl student who, slightly drunk, or just tongue-tied, latched onto a subject that asserted itself, and asked more about Luciana's love of the planes. Nobody had mentioned the wartime presence of planes, the menace and memories they had brought to a span of generations from the twenties to the forties, through Guernica to Nagasaki.

Henri thought of the war plane his uncle had brought him all those years before, unbuilt, ignored, covered in dust and then unceremoniously junked, most of its parts still trapped in their trellis. He thought of all the glue, and its fumes that had probed his mind, opened it, dragged it to the surface of a land full of blinding suns, dust, and hunger, that pleased you till it killed you.

"Planes mean safety, and travel, nowadays, the big world out there." Armen said it easily enough, but Henri saw that his hands trembled. Luciana saw it too. She reached for one, and they watched the planes together, till the little yellow shapes, like airborne toys, vanished around the point.

Eleven

As far as Henri knew, the couple hadn't been in a plane since their trip to gloomy London; he made a mental note to ask them. Very late in the summer that was destined to be his last on the Blue Coast, the wind growing around him and in his bones, he called at their place a few times, then was told by Villemont that 'the upstairs people' had gone on holiday. That was not all he knew, just all he was willing to tell Henri, Henri guessed. The neighbors told him that Armen and Luciana had decided to head for a change of scenery in the late warm weather, and had taken a trip in a car lent to them by a Syrian known as Harry. Henri knew him, vaguely; he had worked the bar at several of the bigger hotels before mysteriously coming into enough money to open his own establishment, a miserable dive beneath the St. Gotthard Hotel in the Arab quarter. Harry was fond of saying, "Squalor? At least it's my own squalor, eh?"

A police inspector of Jules' acquaintance said that the break had got off to a shaky start. A motorbike cop had pulled the couple over not far out of Nice, near the turn-off to Eze. He was too young to know them by reputation, nor, as his days went by in a blur on his speedy machine, even by sight. And anyway, he only ever had half an ear for the older cops' chatter – those men were from a different world, with their cliché tales of the making and losing of fortunes on the spin of a wheel or the turn of a card. The characters in those old tales were all losers to him, walking symbols of the greed that lured people to the Blue Coast and trapped them into crazy things that led to no good. This old couple was a case in point, driving too fast, like a lot of the would-be James Bonds up and down the roads these days – how did they think that was going to end?

The inspector had been on the way to lunch in Cap Ferrat with a film director friend. He was too late to prevent the ticket being issued, as the cop had already entered the details into his book. He pulled over anyway, and greeted them all cordially, waved away the younger man's salute. He shook Armen's hand, and kissed Luciana's, the cop looking on with a mask of patience hiding his irritation.

"I don't see you in the gaming, these days," the inspector observed to Armen, only partly in mischief. Part of it was wistful, he told Jules: you know, he meant, with the vulgar, violent – artless – villains we have to contend with these days. He had a certain nostalgia for a pair like Armen and Luciana; they were a much-missed touch of finesse with their sleights-of-hand and their subtle eye-movements, difficult for either a casino detective or a camera to pick up.

"It's unlikely, unfortunately," Armen almost smiled.

The inspector told Jules, "I saw how old they'd become – he was what, by then, sixty-five? No... Seventy, surely. And Madame, the... wrong side of fifty, of course – and how sick they were. They couldn't hide it."

"They'd spent a lifetime hiding whatever was going on with them," Jules added, when he told this tale to Henri. "All the years I knew them, you could never be sure what they were thinking, about anything. They couldn't do it anymore. I saw it then, too, what the inspector had seen, and what I'd missed, that they no longer had it in them to..."

"To fight?"

"No." Jules looked at Henri, and pitied him, poor dumb junkie. "Anybody can fight," he said, kindly. "No, they could no longer... pretend. That works up a sweat."

That day the inspector saw in Armen a clear hint of Charles Aznavour – sometimes it wasn't there – the look of a weary old fox who'd dodged a lifetime's traps and bullets. He remembered then about the Armenians, and the ordeals they'd gone through in Asia Minor. This man had come intact through times the inspector, who had survived not only Vichy but Occupied France, could not imagine.

"I believe we're barred forever." Luciana enjoyed the mischief the words conveyed, the young cop supposed. He bared his teeth mirthlessly.

"In fact, disbarred," Armen said. It wasn't a pedantic correction, the inspector sensed, but a quote, no doubt, from the Gaming Board's officious report. All the same, it made Luciana's smile vanish for a second, before he caught her eye and she too remembered the ridiculous language they used to put you in your place. She waved a hand, and dismissed them: all those people who sat on boards and passed directives and never had a moment's fun or adventure in their lives, never knew the thrill of the turn of a card as it was halfway to revelation, neither the joy, nor the disappointment.

At first the inspector mistook the gesture for irritation with her husband. They had sometimes been heard arguing fiercely, or so hotel maids and apartment block residents had reported, but were calm by the time they appeared dressed for dinner, for the casino, ready for work. They had hissed curses at each other once as he watched them, he remembered, in the lobby of a Monaco bank. He thought he had spotted a crack in their world at that moment, and tried to peer through it from behind his newspaper, but saw nothing.

"Disbarred," she agreed. She said softly, "Even the most discreet of men can be… disbarred."

"Discretion is no longer a virtue." Armen felt the eyes of the cop and the inspector on him, sensed one frowning, and one nodding. He bent his head gently. "Or so it seems."

"You're right." The inspector thought of the braying villains who now flocked to the coast; their flashy cars and fancy, demanding women, their crass, cutting laughter, and how, when their evening went south, they turned uglier, and louder. "You're better off... retired," he suggested lightly, not wanting his earlier teasing tone to be thought of as mockery.

"We keep busy," Luciana said, with some caution.

The inspector had heard that, without the gaming, the life had gone out of them. Weren't they giving tango lessons in Vence? But he realized that that had to have been a few years back. They were graceful still, straight-backed, handsome – refined: he could imagine the fixed smiles covering their impatience with elephantine, clumsy pupils, seeking the graceful arts and movements of a time that was fast disappearing.

He was stuck on a memory of them years before, at the height of one summer. He had been in a car, the graveyard shift almost over, the sun coming up. He had been hoping there'd be no more holiday season bravado and... idiocy to delay his getting home to sleep. The couple had come out of a casino through the empty outdoor ballroom and bidden their taxi driver to come back in ten minutes. On the dance floor, they had traced the steps of a dance to the music of a band still playing somewhere a little further down the seafront.

"Where are you going?" The cop had waited politely for the older people's conversation to come to a pause.

They looked at each other, said, "Vence," together.

"Well." He handed Luciana the ticket. He looked only sideways at the inspector; it could be stopped, they all supposed, but there was no reason to say why that should be, and no means to do it: these were becoming different times, every aspect of them numbered, docketed, registered. "Thirty kilometers over the legal speed limit," the cop recalled for them. Armen affected the face of a small, contrite boy, and bowed his head. Luciana put her shoulders into an exasperated breath. "Go carefully." He made a tight smile, and bowed briefly to all three before walking back to his bike, mounting it, revving it, and filtering himself into the traffic.

Put so starkly, it sounded like a lot. Henri told Armen, eventually, that even the chauffeur driving that Rolling Stone fellow Bill Wyman had been stopped for doing only twenty over the limit. A cop similar to the one in Armen's story had discovered Bill Wyman in the back, a rock star in blue velvet flares and burgundy slippers, looking like a pantomime dame, and had asked for an autograph, but had still issued the ticket.

"I'm sorry." The inspector had spread hands.

Armen had spread his own, cast his eyes towards Luciana, who was walking back to the car, her head bowed, her legs shaky. He grinned a little self-consciously. He said, in a low voice, "She'll be the death of me."

"Quite honestly, she didn't look well enough to drive," the inspector told Jules. For Henri's benefit, Jules filled in a gap the inspector had either not thought of or, more likely, with that much-admired discretion he and Armen had lamented, had chosen to ignore: Armen had lost his license the year before for a series of frequently-spotted offences, frequently ignored fines, and one unfortunate crash that had spun a car around and injured a driver and one of five children in the car. The tableau at the roadside was a bit of a performance to place Luciana in the driving seat so that Armen could avoid a probable jail sentence.

Nothing, the inspector thought, would be the death of this man. The story was that Armen had escaped the catastrophe of Smyrna by swimming through the fearsome waters of the Aegean Sea, full of fire and oil and mines and sunken ships and corpses, bullets zipping around him to liven up his stroke. Was it just a tale? As if that wasn't enough for one lifetime, every time he had tried to get on with his life, he'd had to flee crises prompted by inter-war fascism in Yugoslavia and Italy, then to contend with ejection from wartime Paris to slave labor programs in Germany, and then was almost forced into repatriation to a Soviet Armenia he had never even visited. Both he and the woman had very narrowly escaped becoming citizens of the Soviet Union, that paradox of a place, still a work-in-progress, and yet already crumbling. Was it all just the kind of wordy sob story heard all over the Blue Coast? The inspector had never liked to ask. Over tables of green baize, on the road to Vence, even in the cells in the police house in Nice, the stories were suggested, and not related, exactly, but all the same were never forgotten.

"I never saw them again," the inspector told Jules, who told Henri, who told me, passing on the essence of that distant, decent man's lament for a way of life that had gone, and taken its cast of characters with it. I pictured the inspector as kindly, and somehow comic, a lesser figure from the Pink Panther films, happy to take long lunches and let the others continue the farce, up and down the coast, cops and robbers chasing the same jewels, and comedy cars going over cliffs.

Twelve

Henri had got the story of their trip in the usual dribs and drabs. He heard it recounted to visitors, each telling of it revealing a new detail, or contradicting one established in his mind.

Armen and Luciana's stop in Vence had been driven by nostalgia, the desire for nothing but sitting in a shaded courtyard and drinking coffee under a window said to have been there since the twelfth century. Then they had headed, at a cautious speed, back to the coast road, and stopped in Cannes, a place they'd not visited in years. They had joked to each other that they had better avoid certain establishments, just to be on the safe side.

They had sat in the car opposite a gaming house now turned into a restaurant. That was a shame, they agreed, this couple who had learned to be glad of the smallest amount of food of the most basic kind, and not quite a tragedy; fancy food was as good a way to lose your money as any.

They had talked about their past encounters with the old police inspector, recalled him wagging a finger, asking them his questions, quoting this law and that regulation, passing them on to colleagues, booking them, reminding them of their upcoming court appearances. They were often let free into stark morning rush hours, dressed still in the formal clothes of the casinos, of the night, drawing looks on the trams and buses, fending them off with resigned smiles, and discussing for the umpteenth time the necessity to sell that asset liberated from a careless Italian Conte, their little de Chirico, at last. They were becoming known up and down the coast by the time they first met the inspector and his colleagues, Jules told Henri, their presence prompting a click of the fingers, an official hand up, their faces sparking life into dull police reports and almost forgotten complaints to the managers of various establishments.

Some of the complainants had described them to the police as a couple in love. Some had dismissed them as a team, employing mercenary precision. They were both, of course. The lovers had built the team, painstakingly, and then they had taken on the appearance of a somberly-clad magician and his gaudy assistant, her fingers full of tiny gestures that gave other people's secrets away, his clothes full of cards in strategic folds, his memory perfect, and full of items others had thought to be their own. They were slight, those people had summed up in their disgruntled statements to the police: she was Latin-looking, they said, and attributed all kinds of nationalities far and wide to her accent. He was either sort of foreign or distinctly Caucasian – they often conjured that up, as if it were a not-quite-respectable word, like hunchbacked. "Like Armenian?" a bored policeman would sometimes prompt, thinking he was about to die of writers' cramp.

"Yes." They would lean forward, excited, a finger raised, glad to be unburdened from their questions. "A bit like Charles Aznavour." Armen had sometimes been mistaken for Charles Aznavour – to his advantage, Jules said to Henri somewhat cryptically – with a distinctly… classical face, and bright, wise eyes, and long thin fingers. She was like a short-haired doll, those plaintiffs said, in some vehemence. At such moments it became plain to the old inspector, at least, that their sense of hurt sprang from their being thwarted from playing with her, that she had turned the tables and played with them. Those big dark eyes, they said indignantly, as if they would have preferred to have been fleeced by a woman with tiny blue eyes, and in her favorite color, it was repeated, in outrage – yellow: sometimes in a dress a little too big for her that, when she leaned over, revealed her collarbone, and breastbone, not cleavage, and sometimes in an elegant linen suit cut for a boy making his first communion.

"You… had to see her," Henri told me, but I didn't. He described Luciana very well, those yellow dresses billowing around her in the breeze, those unusually large eyes, her hair a deep, sleek shade of black. She reminded Henri, he confessed, of women he had seen begging as he walked out to hitch-hike on the edges of grim nineteen-fifties towns in the Midlands of England and in mid-France, famine phantoms who conjured up the newsreels he had seen of the Nazis' Holocaust. "Not doll-like at all." Henri dismissed the words, dismissed all those unimaginative losers. "She reminded me more of a cat. She always seemed self-contained, and very contented, then you saw that she was also on her guard, and that she was able to be all these things at all times. That's what I thought."

She was anorexic, Henri supposed – a word he'd learnt in St. Giles, applied, at least once, to himself. Nobody had heard of such a thing back then, even though women had long been killing themselves slowly with it in the name of that incomprehensible search for the self-hating beauty buried in them. Luciana didn't disdain food, Henri had noticed, but didn't like it much, either, often picked at a salad as a banquet went on around her.

She had the heavy-set beauty of the Dacians and Romans, Henri said, not subtle, but substantial, striking. "Latin and Balkan," he said, and had to explain that for me, a clash of cultures, one rooted in the order of the Roman Empire, the other in the chaos left by the disintegration of another empire, that of the Ottomans. "And the temperament to go with it, by all accounts, quick, and imaginative, but with a downside of paranoia that couldn't be talked down, just had to work its way out in its own time. But a doll? No. Never."

"Doll." Luciana would say the word with scorn, though it was an impression she had sometimes allowed to linger, Henri understood gradually. Such moments opened up a curtain into the couple's world, allowed a glimpse, like in an old mechanical theatre in a fairground. The couple's victims recalled the moment of the blow, when Luciana's eyes glinted, and lines appeared set in her face, the vulnerability gone from it, when she reminded them, "Recall the conditions of this... venture." And she would appeal to Armen, calling one of his variety of names, eliciting a nod, a look that verged on sympathetic, perhaps. It might seem, for a second, as if he would take pity on the victims. Some had said he'd looked to be on the verge of sliding them a chip back over the table, but the next second like he'd just as soon stick a knife in their ribs, a thing he had never done, though, modern life being what it was, and modern people, he had often felt tempted.

Paranoia was one of those words everybody bandied about and overused in the sixties, so I treated Henri's claim about Luciana with skepticism. Armen and Luciana didn't have to be paranoid; the authorities, in a multitude of guises, really were after them for much of their lives. On the Blue Coast, they put up with the private detectives, the investigators who were no more than bureaucrats let out into the fresh air for a day or two, the casinos' bought-and-sold men. The couple laughed as the men spoke of bank accounts and shares. "What we have is what you see," Armen and Luciana said. Those men were too stupid to see the de Chirico on their wall on that occasion. They left empty-handed that time, pointing warning fingers.

The couple didn't have to be watchful of the plodders when they followed them, to Vence, to St. Paul, to Nice, to Monaco, over the border to Ventimiglia, to the market, where they browsed, and stocked up on cheap Italian cigarettes. They stopped at cafés, greeted old friends, and talked about the things on their minds, and always, at some point, pointed over to the watchers. Those men attended to their mineral water, and hid behind their newspapers. Luciana nudged Armen, urged him not to mock them – not to humiliate them, a thing she had a mortal fear of, having seen murder follow mockery during the world war, a horror, she thought, that destroyed the souls of both parties to it. Armen never meant to insult them – they were men doing a dreary job, just like bus drivers, or waiters, or clerks, and to Armen even their labor had its own shabby dignity – but he would cease his jovial pointing. If she excused herself to powder her nose, he would resume his examination of the men and take genuine pity on the boredom etched into their faces, offer the invitation to join him, with that universal drinking hand gesture. He was always refused. She was always relieved.

Their running into the inspector prompted many such memories as Armen and Luciana sat in Harry's car, in Cannes. They laughed a little.

It was early evening by then, people beginning to promenade before dinner, or simply to change shift from work. They saw several men appraising them coolly from afar, a tic of recognition, the consideration of action, peaceable or hostile. The men passed on with the shake of a head and the hint of a grin, the memory of an evening that might still haunt them. Armen and Luciana looked at each other and came close to a laugh, and the words we were terrible, weren't we, sometimes?

They stopped the night in Cannes, at the Albion, safe and cheap although a figment of its former glorious self, they noted. They drove inland, to Perpignan, to Rennes le Chateau, to Carcassonne. They followed the Albigensian trail. They avoided discussing how intolerance, mockery, persecution and sectarian murder had defined it.

Luciana caught something on that trip in Harry the Syrian's car, some bug that made her fearful-eyed and bloodless, made her spasm, and vomit. They found an unremarkable hotel in the unmemorable town of Bram, and stayed there until Luciana confessed to feeling better.

On they went, to Savoie, and to Haut Savoie, to Annecy, where she caught something else.

They had given in to it, and faced home. At a spot specified by Harry the Syrian, shaded by trees not far from the road, Armen had freed the handbrake and pushed the car into Lake Annecy. He watched the bubbles subside, and waited at the roadside until Luciana picked him up in a taxi to bring them to the police station to report the car stolen, and to get an all-important numbered docket to give to Harry for his insurance claim, and then to the train station, and the journey back to Nice.

Thirteen

That autumn most people who knew Armen and Luciana agreed that there was something wrong. Luciana, thin at the best of times, as if she could never overcome the wartime famine imprinted inside her, became thinner, and gave up heels and walked more slowly, more carefully. The couple took in the bad news brought by winter: old acquaintances, friends, enemies, and rivals, fading out and fading away – tales of sudden passings, and hastily-arranged vigils, church services, wakes, and burials. Armen attended the graveyard on the cliff twice, fending off questions about Luciana with smiles he found it easy enough to make, and slight movements of his shoulders.

"His coat looked big on him," some of the mourners agreed afterwards. They moved their own shoulders. "His eyes looked bigger," they said to Jules. "Though still bright – they still have a strange… fire in them."

They stood under the bleached-out trees among the pale stones, watched Armen walk down the main avenue, pass the Gaston Leroux tomb and disappear around a corner, the brown leaves falling after him.

Fourteen

Armen faced the walls of the apartment, tired of the sight of the dump, made sad, for some reason, by the view of the sea, and the leaden light over the Bay of Angels. There was no color at all in the late afternoon, except, finally, a small yellow plane, whose putt-putting claimed his attention as it made its way around the coast, followed two minutes later by its companion.

He told Henri that he would wake Luciana, and tell her the planes would be by again. She always agreed to get up, to be propped up in the chair by the balcony. By the time the first plane came by again, she would often be sleeping again.

"Tired?" Henri said, feeling stupid.

"Yes."

"Exhaustion?"

"Yes." Armen didn't look at Henri, just pointed a finger, nodded. "Exhaustion. I think you're right."

"She… likes the planes." Henri still felt stupid.

"Yes."

The neighbors looked in, but kept a distance, and offered their advice only if it was sought. It usually wasn't. Anina Delessena lived a few doors down in the nearby block, a woman originally from the place she insisted on calling Konstantinopolis, though Istanbul had long planted itself firmly over it. Her ancestors, she told Henri, went back to the ragged aristocracy of the Byzantine Greeks. He could only agree that that was some proper distance, all right, drawing from her a sharp look. She brought exquisitely delicate baked goods, a home-made lemon liqueur, and morphine, sometimes, from some mysterious source, for Luciana. For Armen alone, she brought a shared history, unspoken in the main but always conjured up in some way, alluded to in clichés or throwaway gestures: the dreaded Turks, the good times in Smyrna – a place in which she regretted never having set foot – and a love of rebetiko, the vanished music of Greek taverns.

Gregory Polkowski was thoroughly French, despite the confusion of his names. He brought dark beer which he never offered to anybody, and drank it with studied absorption. He amused Armen and Luciana with tales from his work in the Inspectorate of Municipal Buildings, his gossip that a famed ex-film star was about to be evicted, or that such-and-such a local magnate was about to be hit for back taxes, which would precipitate a scuttling return to his native Persia. "Exotic," he said. "Eh?"

Luciana said later that she'd thought, no, not to a Dacian, but nodded.

Gregory brought his assurances, too, that the building in which they lived was sound; he'd looked up the drawings, and the reports. "What about the water hammer?" Luciana brightened up to ask him, and he tapped his nose, hinting at permitted irregularities from which nearly everybody had come out smiling.

Their other regular visitor was Emilie Brun, from the local hair salon. She had given Luciana's hair its monthly crop and color ever since the couple had moved there. It was a long time since Luciana's hair had been truly dark. "Not jet black," Emilie suggested. "A lighter shade?" She looked from Armen to Luciana.

Luciana said, "Is there such a thing as a lighter shade of black?" Everybody laughed. Emilie brought her expertise into play to suggest shades upon shades upon shades emerging into more shades, an almost-tangible dark rainbow. A kinder shade, she had meant, but refrained from saying so.

She bit her lip. She caught sight of a line of blood that emerged alarmingly from Luciana's nose, wiped away quickly by Armen. She stopped herself from observing that Luciana's face was too white already, and that black hair in any shade would only heighten its pallor, and make it… deathly.

They were all looking at her, expectantly.

Don't let me say that word, Emilie said to herself. She looked around to spy Henri with his gaze fixed on her, his usual easy grin on his face. The junkie, she remembered, shacked up with a princess, she thought, or a countess, was it? Some la-di-da lady, anyway. He hung out with the Rolling Stones at Villefranche, people said, and had borrowed David Niven's fancy car and had crashed it on the road to Eze – or was it Sean Connery's? Only an idiot would choose to steal and crash James Bond's car…

Henri pursed his lips. That made her think she'd spoken out loud. Don't let me be a fool, and say that word, she made her voice say in her head. Why was he looking at her like that – that junkie fool – putting her off like that. She had a flash of anger, then saw the contentment on his simpleton's face, that of some faithful dog, easily pleased. She forgave him. She got her scissors out of its pouch, snip-snipped in the air, grinned at the junkie, grinned at Armen, and at Luciana, showing a strip of her upper gum – a thing some people found endearing, and some found ugly, she had noticed – and told Luciana brightly, "You're going to look lovely."

Henri had read Emilie's mind, an unwanted miracle of perception. Whatever he had seen in Emilie's face had revealed the word deathly to him. He had thought about that moment for years by the time I met him, and still couldn't quite understand how he'd worked it out from all that talk of shades of black. He had made his face still, doing his own internal swearing of oaths against his features betraying his thoughts. He had looked at Luciana once she had submitted to Emilie's ministrations, her closed eyes, the wrinkle in her forehead that, when it moved, revealed jolts of pain.

Armen drew Henri into conversation, and into contented laughter. Henri drank a lemon liqueur, asked, "Is this the one the Greek lady is always threatening me with?" He got a laugh in return from Armen, who was busy making Turkish coffee in a tiny saucepan – "Like a doll's house cauldron," Henri said. Emilie and Luciana watched them, contented in their own ways.

"Oh – oh, it's… grit." Emilie made a face. She had been persuaded to try that infernal coffee, once – never again. "They are drinking grit – tarmac."

"Don't let Anina hear you call it Turkish coffee," Luciana warned the men. "It's Greek coffee when Anina is here," she explained to Emilie and Henri.

Henri said to me, years later, "There was a whole, bitter… world in that comment. I knew a bit about the

history of it by then, Greeks, Turks, wars of independence
– genocide. But it was that comment that made me realize
how these things just linger on and... fester. It made me
think how people like Armen could forgive all they
wanted, but he was in the minority. It depressed the hell
out of me, to be honest."

The thought formed a cloud at the back of his mind
that day, a particularly clear one, overlooking the Blue
Coast. He joined Armen in squinting and pointing at the
ships on the sea. They traced the airliners' graceful
trajectories, their livery defined sharply by the low sun as
they neared the airport, bringing hopefuls to the Bay of
Angels, perhaps for Armen and Luciana, and now Henri,
to meet on a café terrace, with whom they would make
throwaway conversation.

Emilie made some of her own. She sensed a silence,
between herself and Luciana, and from the two men. She
filled it, plucked up the courage to ask Henri about the
car story. "Was it James Bond's car?" she asked, and
teased out more laughter. "Or the Pink Panther's?"

Henri showed genuine puzzlement. They all
believed him when he said he had no idea where that
story had come from. Emilie liked him a little more for
that – it was a good tale in which to have turned down a
role. Their laughter petered out.

The thought struck Henri that they had all run out of throwaway conversation, and for good. Perhaps it had strayed out of his sudden depression, that notion of no forgiveness; so it was with whatever was ailing Luciana. There was no forgiveness in the grip of that dread disease whose name had only ever been whispered in his family. He drank as much as he dared of his Ottoman coffee, and drained his little glass of Byzantine liqueur, and said he had to go. "I didn't want to bring them all down," he told me, still affected, I could tell, by the realization that there was something terribly wrong, and its revelation that day in Armen's and Luciana's apartment as Emilie pondered a word to avoid, although it was the most apt one.

"Did you borrow James Bond's car?" I decided to check.

Henri seemed pained by the question. I was off night shift, and perhaps it hadn't been a quiet one, somebody dead of some geriatric misery, and I'd had to clean up after them and ready a bed for some other walking corpse, and didn't want Henri to bring me down, either. I may not have been in the mood for one of his stories that rambled on with no ending. Perhaps I just wanted my own bed badly. I was nineteen; perhaps I was just being playful, or cruel.

As to the car story, Henri said it wasn't he who had borrowed it, but the countess, either maliciously or simply misguidedly – he didn't know. She had managed to drive it from Cap Ferrat to St. Paul while out of her mind on something-or-other, miraculously avoiding hitting anything or anybody. Henri had driven it back, he remembered, and in some wonder; all these incidents were by then hidden deep in his mind, were almost like déjà-vus from a life he hadn't lived.

I said, "Yeah, but whose car was it?"

"It had no fancy gadgets," he brightened up and said. "No ejector seat, or machine guns, or anything. So I guess it was David Niven's. I still dumped it outside Sean Connery's place, though."

Fifteen

It was partly the whispered naming of the gritty coffee that revived in Henri a dormant curiosity about the mention of Smyrna. As much of their time was convivial, there never seemed to be a good moment to switch the talk from trivia and light heartedness, and turn it towards the darkness that often lay behind Armen's Aznavour eyes.

In gentle fits and starts, Henri steered the conversation towards a night that was orange outside, full of sparks and shouts and wails and gunshots, tramping and running feet, the grind of artillery being moved and positioned, and the violent wrench of wood and masonry as it split apart and fell. There was the troubling rumor that the Greek Patriarch had been lynched by a mob stage-managed by a Turkish pasha, too absurd to be true, and then too absurd not to be; it was passed around in and out of the sounds of the mêlée, the bright night and the smell of burning, and was forgotten, no longer relevant.

"For some years," Armen told Henri. "Even young men had stopped expecting to die in their beds of old age.

The Great War was over in Europe – certainly, but not in the Balkans, and not in Anatolia. The bullets would get you, or starvation, the fire, or the water." His laugh always startled Henri, who wriggled in his seat, seeking some platitude he could answer with a non-committal nothing of his own. He was English, he was always reminded, and cripplingly unequipped to talk about occupation, and conflagration, the mass movements of displaced populations, and about genocide. Armen laughed again, clapped Henri's shoulder, and said, "Don't look so worried, young man. I'm old, as you can see, and my bed is not so far away when I need it."

The water heals, Armen remembered agreeing with Luciana. He raised a finger to bid for Henri's patience. They were swimming off the rocks up the coast from Villefranche, a long time before, a September day, freakishly hotter than either were able to remember. Luciana had cut her foot on something. He had urged her to dip it back into the water. And what it doesn't heal, he remembered thinking, it conceals.

It was the water that had concealed Armen at Smyrna. It became a grave for most of those who swam out to the boats. Later, people said the Turks had sabotaged the crafts in Smyrna harbor. That was probably true, of some of them, at least; mathematics did for the rest of them, a great number of people in vessels meant only for a small number, the mocking slapstick of it.

People would say anything, of course, and later came the claim that the British ships, their bearded jolly jack tars helpless on their decks, had been bribed to turn away – it was against the popular notions of British fair play, and, again, Armen had no way of knowing, nor time to hang around to find out. At the age of twenty, he was a practical man, who had worked in the marine insurance business for a year, and knew that anything outside the limits of the risk was not worth considering.

Because of a gamble he had taken with that insurance company's money, he had spent two years in jail; the risk had been acceptable, or so he had thought at the time. His little venture had been perfect in theory, a quick investment, a quick return with interest, the original funds back in the company coffers before anybody would notice, let down only by the loose tongue of a fellow-conspirator while drunk. Armen had sworn never to drink alcohol. He had sworn to work alone in the future. He had also sworn revenge on his one-time partner-in-crime. He remembered the words of one Dimitrios Makropoulos, a waterfront fig-packer, who told him, "Your heart's got to be in murder, more than in any other act." It was the word of a man who should have known; Makropoulos was later wanted for murder in every state in the Balkans. For at least a few months of nineteen twenty, part of Armen's imprisoned heart was devoted to nothing else.

As luck had it, Armen's one-time partner and betrayer was soon transferred to the same prison, caught out in another half-hearted petty crime. Armen took the earliest opportunity to guide his home-made blade to the man's jugular, then at the crucial moment decided that the man's wriggling, and pissing, and saying his prayers, was revenge enough. Not enough of his heart had been in murder, it was clear. He had looked the man in the eye, put the knife away and pointed a finger, unable to say anything. It occurred to him to declare that, irreligious as he was, revenge was not worth his soul, but it was a thought for himself; that would be his revenge, not to share this truth with this worthless specimen of a man.

In Smyrna Jail, Armen had become strong, his pale, office-stunted body becoming brown and wiry as he ferried stones and bricks to build another wing of the prison to receive all the feckless, luckless, drunken, loose-tongued men of the future Smyrna was not destined to have.

The night the city burned brightest, Armen had not swum since he was a child, up along the Aegean before the war from the beach the Ottomans called Uluja, his parents hiding him and his sister under a parasol from the fearsome sun. He thought of them that night: his father, kindly even under the weight of the jailbird shame Armen had brought on him, his nervous mother, stoic in the face of that shame, forcing herself into trembling composure, and his gentle, beautiful, forgiving sister. He thought of them, that night and for all the other nights of his life, gone, he had to guess, in the all-consuming fire or the polluted water. He didn't know where, and couldn't think where, could think only of what to do next.

The hinterland was deadly, he knew, populated by the enemy, with their munitions, their mercenaries, their vengeance. Armen had slid into the water off a small jetty, the varnish bubbling on it with the heat, all that remained of his one-time employers the Varoushians' waterfront mansion. He kept near the harbor shore, dived to the harbor floor whenever he heard gunshots, avoided being impaled by bullets and yet nearly decapitated himself or lost a limb on the sunken junk below. He swam a long way – an impossible way, for hours and hours – around the bay, to the area known to the Turks as Karshiyaka. He pulled a dead child out of a skiff, buried him in the water, then was buoyed into the mist, rank with the stench of a city passing into history and ashes. The smoke followed him for a long way out, clinging to his clothes, to his hair, his hands. Bodies bumped the craft, and startled him, and kept him awake, this ghost of human agency.

Water had not saved Armen in Smyrna – no, prison had, with the physique its labor had forced on him, and the attitude it had instilled in him. Milk-white clerks were not going to survive the night around him with its ordinance, and its conspiracy of elements: that fearsome fire, the deadly water, the wind that sought to blow him back to the inferno, the earth that would have received his cremated remains. He was going to beat them all.

He lay back on the boards, exhausted. He levitated, or so he imagined, delirious, slavering, his lungs glowing with coals, he fancied, whenever he raised a hand to his mouth in the way mannered people sought to hide a cough to spare onlookers from germs. Water was paradoxical, he had often had the idle thought, and there it was again, all around him. Water was death, in Smyrna, filled up the lungs, and burst them, but it was also life; it parted under the force of the hands and feet, and of wooden oars, aided propulsion, and escape. It cleansed, and yet it was filthy stuff.

He awoke, he coughed, this time without hiding it, forced the stuff up from his lungs with impossibly long breaths out, which held him hostage to the point at which he felt he would be unable to breathe in again. He forced that air out and eased it in. He rowed, kept thinking of the paradox of the water, and the world to which it would carry him. He became fixed on it, became crazy with it. His mouth seemed to have no moisture left in it, and his last thought was that – the comedy of it – for lack of water he was going to end his days in the water. Then he was back in the future, spluttering, manhandled, one of those bearded British matelots from the Senior Service cigarette pack pulling him onto a patrol boat by a hook and a hand, splashing clean water onto his face, and then ladling it gently down his swollen, soot-blackened throat.

Armen told Henri that he often sensed the story rising in him, studded with details he had forgotten – perhaps it was the black dirt outlining the intricate rope patterns in the sailor's lanyard, unrecalled until now – and he could never quite put it to rest. Even with the inconsequential minutiae of its genocide aided by the pitiless elements, the story was a celebration of life. When he shared it with Henri, there would be the odd phrase that stood out, and made Luciana shake her head, raise a hand to interrupt, guide a question to her lips that she forced back, thinking better of it, thinking it ought to be left where it lay, in the filthy water of the Aegean.

Sixteen

"I was bitten by a spider," Luciana said out of the blue. Armen remembered the evening, he told Henri, because of the Turkish coffee cups, and the liqueur glasses, abandoned on the balcony table, and some stray clumps of hair on the floor, missed by Emilie as she swept up after Luciana's cut and dye. Luciana had been sleeping deeply, and in some agitation, it seemed to Armen, fists clenched then relaxed, a frown lining her forehead, her nose twitching.

Armen, across the little room, was almost asleep himself, a book flopped over on his lap. He looked up, and, a little alarmed, said, "When?"

She didn't know. He went and sat on the Moroccan leather pouffe by the bed, and looked up into her face. Her eyes were wide open, but there was something about her that spoke of sleep; Henri had seen her do that, had never been able to make out for sure which state she was in. Her whispers revealed to Armen that she meant the swastikas she'd seen after fleeing from Chisinau to Bucharest, when the Germans moved in to steal any of their Romanian ally's resources they had left, and hung their four-meter flags from wherever they could. Armen remembered a long-lost conversation they'd had, in which Luciana recounted how she'd had to convince an elderly relative that the swastikas weren't spiders, and could do her no harm.

All the same, her report of a bite had sounded an alarm. Armen said, "A bite – where?"

"I can't remember." She held a hand up, made a weak fist whose fingers didn't quite close it in, and turned it. "On a finger, I think."

"It wasn't a wasp?" he said. "A bee?"

"No. They do no harm. They guard the coast. They make me feel safe."

"It's just a stray memory," Henri assured Armen, when he got there. He ran his hand over his face. "I have them myself. I sometimes don't know what's happened," he confided to Armen, "and what hasn't – not really, not… with the certainty I used to have. It's not the morphine, anyway," he said.

Anina Delessena's supply of morphine was intermittent, and Henri had taken over supplying it, got it not from some shady reprobate but from one of the countess's more respectable contacts at a pharmacy in Cagnes. "The morphine is good. And she's not at a stage where it'd mess up her mind, man."

Armen dreaded word of such a stage, but felt reassured. There was something about Henri that made Armen believe he knew what he was talking about in this instance.

She's old, Henri could have said, and he wouldn't have meant it in a sniping way. He refrained, anyway. She's sick, he could have said, but that was too obvious. She's weak, he could have said, but that was also obvious, and at the same time a revelation; he didn't even want to think it himself. Her brain is coping with all the weird stuff, he pondered saying, holes appearing, things crawling out of them and back in before she can get a handle on them.

"She's… in pain, anyway." That much was clear. Henri forgot the rest, and administered the stuff in head-bent silence.

Armen woke in the night, he told Henri, alerted somehow by a deeper quality to the darkness outside: a power cut on the hill. Luciana slept peacefully, or so it seemed, the rasp of her breath far away, and yet amplified.

He sought the light, but hesitated over lighting a candle. He had an aversion to naked flames, and avoided them if he could.

Henri told me that at all such times of sudden awakening, Armen remembered Smyrna, and I said, impatiently, like the mouthy teen I was, "Of course he did," as if I were suddenly an expert.

Armen sat up late in his chair, watching Luciana go through the labor of sleep tunneled with opiates. Then he was no longer watching, but himself asleep, a paradoxical thing he realized only on waking again.

Wild dogs woke him, barking out on the dump, howling at the darkness brought by the cut in power. He saw them sometimes in the daylight, and couldn't help but compare them to Henri: their lives were a bit of a wreck, but there they went, nimble, optimistic, curious, ineffably friendly. "Yeah, that's me, for sure," Henri agreed, too enamored of all those complimentary words not to.

It was impossible to tell whether the hounds were enjoying the mystery of the darkness around them, howling and barking with excitement, or fearing and hating it. They smelt the cats who came near, Armen guessed. He imagined the cats creeping up on the dogs in the deep darkness, slyly thrilled at their proximity, anticipating the crowning moment of their feline game when, with the lights back on after a second of halogen buzz, the dogs looked up and saw those glowing eyes and feared that they were trapped in a circle of lions and tigers, jaguars and cougars, and howled in anguish before the cats, the comedy of their work achieved, scattered.

When Armen woke fully, he recalled that it was Henri who had actually seen the tableau of the mischievous power-cut cats frightening the dogs on the dump. He had fallen asleep one warm night in a chair out on the balcony and Armen hadn't had the heart to wake him and banish him. He had an idea it had been a tactical sleep, anyway, the countess having relatives visiting, who didn't want a junkie cluttering up their little château, the poor, precious things. Henri knew the value of a story, Armen thought, and had offered the tale of the mischievous power-cut cats in return for his uncomfortable bed, the crick in his neck and the cramp in his junkie joints, and the breakfast to which Armen had treated him.

But he didn't need to bring stories, Armen wanted to tell him; he had brought the morphine, after all. "Proper stuff," Henri had assured Armen, as he always did, and, as always he had dosed Luciana with it, and had – or did Armen imagine this? – suggested that there might come a time when… more might be required.

"More?" Armen had put on his face of mild-mannered enquiry, but Henri had seen a panic flare at the back of his friend's eyes. He had raised his breakfast croissant in his long white fingers, and bitten into it with gusto, exactly like a man who only remembered to eat every few days. He had repeated to Armen that everything was going to be fine, each man dismissing and clinging to the few words.

Seventeen

"He wanted me to flog him some," Henri told me. It was almost an afterthought. Henri, who was nothing if not frank about the many errors of his ways, looked a little sheepish for the first and last time. "For himself. I mean, he wouldn't touch her kosher morphine, of course."

I said, "Some... what?" I was genuinely puzzled.

"Diamorphine." One of the older doctors at St. Giles insisted on calling heroin by its more obscure name, in a refusal, Henri had surmised, to be drawn into the counter-culture and its terrible habits. Henri was ambiguous, partly approving of the doctor's stance, and partly feeling singled out as an embodiment of those despised habits. I thought the doctor was just being funny – the words diamorphine addict having the same Daily Telegraph ring as popular music beat group – but in any case Henri echoed the word, depending on how he was feeling, as either a share in the disdain or a mark of respect.

"I said he shouldn't." Henri held helpless hands up. "He was – how old?" He thought about it. "Sixty-eight, seventy, maybe? He'd got to that age without using anything like that. He said he wanted to see what she was seeing. He wanted to go where she was going, he said. I said to him, it's not magic, man. I said he wasn't going to see unicorns. It's sepia, if anything."

Old photos, Henri told Armen, just like old photos, that was all. He said, "There's a reason we don't have sepia any more. We have Kodachrome, man – we have full color."

I said, "What did he say to that?"

"Oh." Henri bit his lip. "He went off on one of his… tales."

Armen remembered sepia, of course, the photos on family mantels, on walls in the houses of merchants, of schoolteachers, civil servants, the well-to-do, while the Ottoman peasants around them still believed that a photo could steal their souls, imprison them in frames for eternity. He remembered them on the walls of Varoushian's Marine Insurance offices, a roll call of stiff men in absurd formality – their own form of imprisonment, in their Ottoman fezzes and western suits and wing-collars. It was all part of the vanity of people who thought they'd always have mantels on which to place trophies and trinkets, and walls around them.

He remembered the colors of Smyrna, all of them, a whirl of them, exploding finally into orange and black, and little in between. He remembered a neighbor, one of those everyday merchants, slumped against a wall, his eyes wide open and jumping with the flames. There was a strange mark on his face in the shape of a figure of eight in a brilliant shade of red, nothing supernatural, he supposed; it had become commonplace that night: a jagged exit wound made by a large-caliber bullet.

Drawing an eight of diamonds or hearts had forever recalled the sight to Armen.

"He had a tendency to do that," Henri said to me. "I don't think I realized it at the time. If he didn't want to discuss something, he didn't say so straight, he just blocked it out with some... story that was meant to explain what he was thinking about, or his reason for something – a sort of... illustration."

"Sepia suits me fine," Armen had told Henri.

"I made it weak," Henri said. "I told him he'd throw it all up in a few minutes, anyway. You always do, first time. It's a massive shock to the system, after all. He had a strong constitution, though, I suppose."

"It wasn't your fault," I said.

"They were fine when I left them. They were fine."

"I'm sure they were, Henri."

"No – they were, though. He started talking about the cats."

"Cats?"

"The ones on the dump, how they freaked the dogs out, creeping up on them in the dark. And, you know, he was telling me a story I'd told him... I mean, it didn't matter. I was just going, yeah, sure, man, that's funny. Anyway, he said he was going to tell her about them, when she woke up. He wasn't... babbling, or anything. He was talking lucidly, you know? Calm, but looking at me closely to make sure I understood the story – the cat story – my own stupid cat story. He seemed really... bothered that I might not find the humor in it. And all I was thinking was, I know. But really, I swear."

"What?"

"They were fine when I left. They were."

It was summer, early morning, Camberwell Green. We were on a park bench opposite Kember's chemist. We were waiting for it to open so that Henri could get his methadone, and be consumed into the sepia it supplied. A one seven one bus went by – mine, as I'd moved up to Waterloo by then. I wished I was on it. I was dog-tired. I had to stay there with Henri, though, just a while longer, so I could tell him I believed he'd done the right thing that evening an age before on the Blue Coast. And I did, but it didn't matter whether I did or not: the important thing was to keep saying so.

We'd seen the chemists clatter Kember's shutters up and go in, fifteen minutes before opening. I heard the ring of the shop's customer bell, and nudged Henri, his eyes drawn to a plane high above us. I raised a thumb. I walked across the road with him, left him to take his place in the ragged queue of dodgy early-morning shoppers, their scripts clutched in their hands.

"They were fine," he said.

"I believe you."

"That last night – they were fine."

"And what, though?"

I wanted to ask him again, but his business preoccupied him, so I walked off to get my bus.

Eighteen

They went out and walked, that last night, or so Henri had to suppose. He said, "I couldn't help thinking how Armen pulled that last night out of his hat in Smyrna, and all those other horrible times and places he lived through, saved it up. And Luciana, too – extracted herself out of a country that just… disappeared under her feet. She put her last night off, too. And what did they do?"

I was silent, frustrated, on the verge of a certain scorn and insolence that Henri sometimes brought out in me. Henri was supposed to be telling this tale, not me. I said, "Don't ask me."

"They… wasted it," he said.

In St. Giles, I'd seen people go suddenly, move their heads in a last bow, widen their eyes momentarily, sink into themselves, fall off the edge of the world and never come back up. The truth is that everybody's last night on earth is a waste; most people would rather do anything else than die. I said so to Henri, and said, "You're… hard on them, Henri."

His eyes blazed, then went dull, and he reverted to his usual change of subject. "They were fine when I left them."

I understood that. It didn't stop him saying it.

Luciana and Armen walked out into the blue-tinged night, everybody supposed. Nobody saw them go. Emilie Brun could see the entrance to Villemont's motor yard from where she lived, and had often seen them in and out, at all times of the day and night. But not that night. Anina Delessena was often out with her insomnia, walking it off, down a mile to the coast road to get a bit of sea air in her lungs, and she had often met them – but not that night.

All the neighbors had accompanied them at times on at least part of their walks, so had their own ideas of which streets they might have taken. Henri traced them all. They told him nothing. Scraps of conversations came back to him, of all the things he'd learned from them, all those events, all those places, all those... horrors. But they told him nothing. He traced the streets again. Nothing.

"The cats know," Emilie had said glumly to Henri, and to Gregory Polkowski. She'd pointed at the cats, a gang of them down the street at their idle business in the weak sunshine. "The cats saw them."

She forgot herself, Henri thought. It was too early for jokes. He saw her hooded eyes, her down-turned mouth, a strand of her thick dark hair trapped in her teeth, saw that she wasn't joking, just… thinking out loud. He said, "They're not telling."

"Cats know everything."

"If we could ask them…" Gregory joined in.

"Go ahead." Henri was sick of it. He stood up, walked off, called back, "You can ask. You can ask all you like."

Armen in a suit, Henri supposed. A bit late in the year for linen, perhaps – summer-weight wool, he thought Armen had called his autumn threads. Too early for even a light coat. And one of his bright ties all done up with a fancy Windsor knot. Luciana in one of her yellow dresses, he supposed, billowing, showing off her slender, shiny shins, and her narrow little feet, the sides of her pumps spreading like bellows as she walked. He imagined them under the streetlights, losing form briefly in the darkness, then taking it on again in the spread of the next light. It was an impossible view, he kept thinking – impossible, because nobody had been there to see it.

They stopped under the trees, he supposed further, to catch a breath. He examined them: dusty evergreens in need of a sprinkling of rain to bring their color back. Or they stopped to give Luciana a chance to pull out the inhaler a doctor had given her, a decongestant, they'd told Henri, but he suspected it was even more morphine.

Slow progress, he imagined, the night around them tinged blue, welcoming, engulfing, a chill to the paving stones, a crunch to the fallen leaves, an augury of autumn that they noted. Then they passed on, unseen.

Luciana had been unable to speak much above a pained whisper, Henri remembered. Armen had in turn adopted a whisper of his own. "Nobody would have heard them," Henri spelled out to me. "I thought about it when I tried to plot their route, and follow it. I thought about knocking on doors, asking people if they'd seen them, or even just heard them outside the window, down in the street."

"Why didn't you?" I asked him.

He looked at me. I kept up the same look of dogged enquiry. He shook his head. I kept it up. I was young, and not stupid… exactly… but wanting all I saw before me on my own terms. I genuinely didn't understand that those conservative Nicois people would have taken one look at a door-knocking junkie and set their dogs on him before they found out the sadness and desperation behind his mission.

Armen and Luciana walked – that was all Henri, and anybody, knew. They went out, and they walked. He ran through it time and again: Armen selecting a tie, standing at the mirror to fasten it, and appraise it, asking Luciana to say for the thousandth time that she liked it. "All telling me nothing," he said, and yet, in his dreams and daydreams, in the visions granted to him by opiates, he couldn't help but run through it all, over and over, and there he was, in Camberwell, an age later, seeing if anything more would come to him.

"They were fine," he told me.

"You mentioned that."

He put on a face I didn't see very often, earnest junkie seeking approval. I patted his arm. I said, for what felt like my thousandth time, "I believe you, Henri."

It was the last night of the future each had wangled, from the deadly waters of the Aegean, from the fiery fields of Bessarabia, and... they walked. That was all, the blue night closing around them, refusing to let them go.

"There was a thing she used to say," Henri said. "About how having a mystery was better than solving one."

"True." I'd never thought about it.

"No. No. It's not."

"Hmm." I thought about it again, and said, "That's true... too."

Henri went from being a confidant of the couple to being just another onlooker – circumstances didn't respect friendship, or intimacy – subject to the mystery's tyranny, frustrated in its darkness. In time, he was reduced to being a reluctant teller of the story. "I was never… artistic," he said. "You know all those people who say there's a book in them?" He shook his head sadly. "Not in me. I never wanted to write a book or paint a picture. You know? But I sometimes wished I was able to, so I could say what runs through my mind. Or what was left of it, down on the Riviera."

I said how he was doing all right – he was. I saw the tale as he added to it, like in a film I'd watched again and again. He twisted his mouth to one side, turned his eyes down, blank. It was true, though: he was a teller of tales, like a film director at times, one with a massive budget, changing his mind, making sense of the story from a different angle, one that pleased him more on any given day. In that way, perhaps he was more like a singing bard, passing on the story he knew, and making up the bits he didn't, sensing that his audience preferred events, any events, to silence or speculation. I was the audience. I took liberties with my status. I quizzed Henri mercilessly, sometimes, and scoffed – pitilessly – and laughed, said come on, how can you know that – and infuriated him, like any stupid teenager. He was right, though: I wanted the story from him, in any form, with any twist in it, and found it hard to accept him saying I don't know.

"They went for a walk," I repeated, and tutted.

"That's it."

The couple were fine that night when he left them – okay, I got it – and they walked, out of Henri's life, but, paradoxically – a word I didn't know when Henri told me all this – they walked into mine, steadfast, and unstoppable.

Nineteen

Their disappearance wasn't noticed for a day or so. Villemont was used to their nocturnal lifestyle. They had often slept all day while he worked, arising only in the mid-evening. In this way, he wouldn't see them for weeks. They had often gone away, too, of course, though he usually looked over the car for them, as a favor, before they set off, tweaking a bolt here, topping up the oil, the water, moving the fan belt a few millimeters this way or that, making this much of it, or that. "They are quiet, of course," he told Emilie Brun when she came in to call. "And if they weren't..." He nodded back to the whine of a drill, the beating of a panel, the inane chatter of his teenage apprentices. "I wouldn't know. Oh, the savage came by."

"Who?"

"The junkie."

He accepted her challenge when she tried to stare the word back at him.

She said, "Henri."

Villemont repeated the name dismissively.

"He's not so bad." Emilie was stung on Henri's behalf – she didn't really know why. She bit her lip, debated with herself whether she ought to speak out of turn, then decided to do so. "He brings her morphine," she said.

Villemont went all petit-bourgeois France for a second – utterly scandalized – and swept the word away with a hand. His face fell from its high dudgeon only when Emilie told him of Madame Luciana's illness. He fell quiet, and listened, and punctuated each thing she said with an oh-oh from the back of his throat.

"The hospital." Villemont was keen to make good his bad grace. He drove Emilie to the Hospitalier Universitaire. She watched the city out the car window, drizzled with oily rain, miserable, its people silhouetted and distorted, disheartened in their very steps, on pessimistic errands that ended only in a gloomy retracing of those steps. Villemont regretted having to leave her there; he had an urgent job on for the mayor, he said, but she absolutely had to come to see him later, and tell him how she'd got on. He waved money at her for a taxi home, and, after a haughty hesitation somewhat ruined by the realization that she had only a few francs on her, she accepted it.

She found no trace of Luciana at the Universitaire. She traipsed to a few of the other hospitals, but found no trace of the couple, nobody... only, at the last, a tiny, private one tucked up the hill near the Beaux Arts Museum, Henri. He looked lost, and looked white, looked at the wall, at the floor, full of the news that his fragile countess had not long before died of an overdose. The family had arranged for her body to be removed in a shiny car from an upmarket undertaker's. A relative had summoned up the courtier's aristocratic disgust to hand Henri the few grams of heroin found in the countess' handbag, and had made it plain that it was a parting gift. They never wanted to hear from him again.

Henri intoned this new episode of his story somewhat matter-of-factly, Emilie thought, his words enunciated slowly, and almost elegantly. That was what he was always like, she remembered: unfazed by anything. It was his nature. She looked into his eyes. He was dying inside, she could see. She was perturbed. She had to revive him – God, she had to bring him back, through that drizzling, miserable world outside. He nodded at each slight sound she made, as if he knew the words she couldn't trap long enough to make any sense, and was acknowledging her intent.

Emilie waited as Henri did some business in the toilet, and came out bright-eyed but floppy, unsteady on his feet to begin with, and then slipping into movements that reminded her of a... squirrel – yes, that was it: he moved as if he weighed nothing, and with an alertness fixed on some event only he could see, in a place beyond her horizon. He began to tell her a story about Bill Wyman's driver – yes, yes, the Stone, no, not the singer, one of the others – and the time he had lent Henri Bill Wyman's car without telling Bill Wyman, and Henri had ground its delicate wing gently into a concrete post by a garage in Villefranche.

So… not James Bond's car, she thought, later, remembering his earlier story, and felt slightly cheated.

"I was parking it, you see, only temporarily, but it… didn't stop where it was supposed to. I was looking out the wrong window, because they drive on the other side."

"What?" Emilie was agitated, no longer diverted, back in her mind to the missing Armen and Luciana. "Who?"

"We, I mean. I mean… here."

"What are you talking about?"

"It was hilarious. Everybody thought so." Henri went briefly into a deep study. "Well… it wasn't. But it seemed it at the time."

He was delirious, she supposed. He was mad with grief. She had seen such a thing in a film. "I'm not interested in this… car," she said.

Outside the hospital, Henri pointed towards a whiteish shape in a nearby street, said, "It's there. The car. Bill's driver lent it to me again," he claimed. "I was going to bring her home in it, you see. In the car." He looked keenly at Emilie, making sure she had understood. She nodded, half in a daze. "When the hospital called, I thought she was alive. I didn't realize she was... gone."

"Oh, God." Emilie's mouth flew open, and she covered it hastily. "What a... horror."

"Yes. I was going to bring her back, wasn't I, get her to rest. But now... I can't." He sat down abruptly, arse on the pavement, feet in the road, his Spanish leather boots scuffed and straining, comically straight up from the ground, somehow, though his legs were at an angle. "I cleaned up the apartment," he said. "I thought it'd be a... surprise for her."

Emilie saw his grief again; it was as if some unforgiving monster had taken over his face from inside. She reached out a hand and pulled him up, noting how light he was, the proportionate weight of a squirrel, yes. He twitched like one again, looked up and down the street, patted his pocket to make sure he had remembered his small legacy. He said, "It took almost an hour."

"What did?" She raised a thumb back to the hospital, then realized he meant cleaning the apartment. If it really was, as she had heard, the size of a château, she reflected that he couldn't have got it very clean in that time. The countess might not have been very pleased with it after all.

Henri was not fit to drive, Emilie could see. After some silent debate with herself, she drove them back to Armen's and Luciana's in Bill Wyman's rather scruffy car. It was definitely not a rock star kind of car, but she didn't have much time to expend on disapproval. It was only the second time she had driven in the four years since getting her license. She drove too slowly, and was hooted, drove too fast, and was honked, lingered too long at lights and was hazed, shot through them and was grazed. She was relatively terrified, which kept the foreboding that threatened to engulf her at bay.

The workshop was silent and dark. Villemont and his mechanics had gone home, but he had pinned a note to his door with the phone number of his local bar. They hurried up the stairs and called at Armen's and Luciana's apartment. They tapped on the door, and said tentative hallos, then called the couple's names, and banged the door, making it shake in its frame. Again, Emilie was faced with nothing, no sound, no light, nobody.

Not knowing what else to do with him, Emilie took Henri home with her. She parked him in a corner of the living room, where he sat without moving. She explained his temporary presence to her parents – and his no doubt temporary silence – before calling Anina Delessena to come to collect him.

Twenty

That evening, Henri absented himself in the sometimes frank way of junkies who no longer care what anybody thinks of their weakness, and used some of the morphine he had collected for Luciana, and some of the heroin he had inherited from his countess. Anina Delessena was too busy to be disapproving of her guest; she had already made the search for Armen and Luciana her life's work. Around eleven that night, she called Adie, the landlord, who let her into their apartment. Villemont had also turned up by then, a faint whiff of brewery about him and in the mood for having questions answered. They surveyed the neat, yellow rooms, almost devoid of possessions, noted passports in drawers, a little money too inconsequential to remark upon, empty suitcases on top of wardrobes, the couple's clothes hung on hangers or folded in drawers.

Adie, an agitated middle-aged man whose eyes swum with anxiety and a mild narcotic of some kind, was immediately concerned – possibly about the palaver involved in getting replacement tenants who would be willing to live above a car service garage, Anina

Delessena suspected. She walked back along the street and roused Emilie, and her parents, from sleep, for no good reason, really, Emilie thought at first. Anina had just wanted her to cast a critical eye over Henri, she soon saw. She did so, and they left him in a snoring heap in Anina's spare room, abandoned for the second time that day, but oblivious. Villemont drove them all to the nearest police station.

The police could do nothing, they said. A crime had not been committed, and the vanished pair were adults. "You mean it's their responsibility to report themselves missing?" Emilie asked, and got the coppers laughing, almost gratefully. She drew the special attention of one, a thin local man who looked all of eighteen, with a bony face and wavy dark hair that was too long on one side, his eyes a startling blue. He laughed longer than the other coppers. They in turn laughed at him, and nudged one another as he looked up from his paperwork and his citron pressé, and raised himself a little in his chair to see the deliverer of this comic gem.

"But you can check the hospitals," Anina said. The desk sergeant agreed, and said he would do that, and promised that, if he found the missing pair, he'd tell this seeking pair. Anina believed him. The young blue-eyed man raised himself to his full height, and said he'd take charge of that very thing that very minute. He hitched his trousers, and pulled his jacket from the back of his chair and put it on all in one fluid, impressive movement. He also surreptitiously slipped his feet into his shoes, or so Anina Delessena concluded when she idly inspected the creased backs of them. He came out front to declare his services – there not being any murders to solve, or anything, that evening – and the use of a car, to tour the city's hospitals.

"We have a car," Emilie said, and everybody looked at her. She was going to splutter out excitedly that they had rock star Bill Wyman's car, then decided she'd better not. She didn't quite trust Henri's story, and suddenly wasn't sure what part Bill Wyman had actually played in the donation of his car.

"A car?" she was asked.

"A… what?" she said, and put on a dumb face. She made a recovery in a turn towards Villemont, mumbled something that sounded like garage. Villemont said hastily that he really had to take a step towards his bed – he got up at five thirty every day of his life, he claimed – and to let the cavalry take over, now that they had its attention. The young policeman grinned, said his car would be better than a horse. Emilie thought she ought to confess that she had already been to the hospitals… but said it might not do any harm to go again. And Anina Delessena could take a well-earned rest, then, couldn't she, and keep an eye on… what's-his-name, make sure he didn't do any grief-stricken harm to himself.

"You think so?" Anina did not seem keen on the idea, but resigned herself to it.

"What's-his-name?" The young copper quoted, seemed alert to the presence of a man not far out of the picture.

"But what about the apartment?" Adie wailed.

The police could help him there, the sergeant said. The law was clear: unless he received notice that his tenants were leaving, he was not allowed to evict them, even as a short-term measure. Anina nudged him, said, "Well, at least that's one sure piece of information." Anina believed that a man… or woman… should own their property, and live in it, and be satisfied with it: she didn't approve of landlords. Both Emilie and Adie suspected that she had started enjoying some part of the evening, at last.

"This way, mademoiselle." The copper jingled his car keys, and, as he led Emilie down the steps outside, Anina smiled to hear him asking, "So… this what's-his-name?"

"Yes?"

"What… is his name?"

He's not important were the words he wanted to hear, and Emilie obliged. This got him smiling, and even more eager to please. Anina was convinced that, if nothing else, those hospitals would be checked thoroughly, and that her friends would be back in their apartment very soon.

Twenty One

Adie got his wish, two months on, when a month's rent became due, and was missed for a certain number of days and, it could be assumed, with the full support of some legal definition, was not going to appear. Armen's and Luciana's things were removed from the apartment, some of them to Emilie's, some to Anina's. Henri, who had been flopping in the couple's place from time-to-time, was also removed, looking stoic, and philosophical, with the occasional hint of a faint amusement whose origin only he could know. The apartment stood empty and silent. By day the drills and paint guns whined and chattered, and by night the dogs howled over on the dump, and the cats yowled in return.

Henri was sometimes seen on the coast, on a promenade bench, or up the hill in the Arab quarter, and further up, by the station. He was spotted in Villefranche, at the harbor at Cap Ferrat, and sitting on a stone watching the geyser-like plumes of water forced through the rocks under the lighthouse. He was very visible, I gathered, going about his business, sometimes doing odd jobs around the port, and often in a state of cheerful, weather-worn ruin.

In contrast, it was as if Armen and his intriguing companion had vanished into the blue air. They were discussed, in the newspapers and in the bars, in the casinos, and in the hotels, and in the police stations, too, but not for very long – not long enough, it seemed to Henri. He was stumped by the passing phases of their disappearance and, finally, absence. He was also more frustrated than he could acknowledge that the stories he could tell about them had reached an end.

"Or so I thought." He cursed, softly. "All the things I wished for," he always told me, without fail. "They never did me any good. And this was no exception."

Because one of those little yellow coastguard planes was making a pass over the coast one bright day the following spring, and its pilot, aimless, expecting neither inland fires so early in the year nor nefarious activity on the sea, was able to spare some attention for the unusual. He and his companion were on a training run, just to keep men and machines up to scratch. He waited for sight of his mate, and they prepared to follow one of their regular routes, over Cap Ferrat, to wake up those millionaires, shake their china in their cabinets for them, and then get back to Nice for a bite.

The leading pilot wasn't even using any of his sighting equipment. He was looking out the window. He wasn't very low over the ruined, razed area over the coast by the Haut Cagnes road. He wasn't looking for anything in particular, but caught a glimpse of something out of place. He radioed over to say he'd be going round again, and he did. Amid the debris of the dump, a flash of yellow waved in the stagnant water at its lowest point. He wasn't sure what it was – he didn't dare go any lower.

Back at base, he reported that it looked to him like a woman's dress. A bell rang about a yellow dress. The men in the room slowly voiced recall of a couple's disappearance – the gamblers, wasn't it, the summer-suited man, the woman in yellow, walked off into the night, didn't they, that time – or had they all imagined that – and shouldn't they tell somebody, and… who?

Twenty Two

The coroner's court couldn't establish the cause of death with any certainty. Drowning, its officers assumed, or exposure, perhaps. They were puzzled about the couple's ultimate location, in the deepest part of the dump. They'd lived overlooking it, so it was surely out of the question that they'd been in the habit of visiting it, as if it were some local attraction, or foraging for any of the junk there – if people got rid of something there, it really was clapped out and useless, irredeemable.

Foul play was considered. The couple had for thirty years made a living using a few sophisticated cons aimed at gamblers – "Bad gamblers," an expert witness pointed out, meaning, he had to elucidate for the public gallery, that only the most inept and inattentive gamblers would have fallen for their guile. For years the casinos had lost marginal sums to the couple's tricks, partly due to newly-penniless gamers heading home early, or retiring to the few places they could afford for the rest of their stays, but eventually a new breed of owners had sought every possible sou their investment could return. A few also bleated hypocritically about the principle of the thing.

The couple had been blacklisted at the casinos for some years, and had become increasingly impoverished, living on savings and handouts, and the controversial selling-off of a small painting by Italian master Giorgio de Chirico, contested unsuccessfully in a high-profile court case by the Italian relatives of its one-time owner.

They forgot the flat, it occurred to Henri, as he sat in the public gallery. He knew that Armen and Luciana had won a flat one time off some luckless visitor, in some… run-down corner of London – the words seemed to chime with him; he had never heard of Camberwell, he supposed, back then on the Blue Coast, had no knowledge of its hospital beds, its celebrated but unlovable patch of green. He had long wondered if the London flat tale had been just that – an entertaining yarn. Or whether they'd sold it long before, spent the money wildly, lost it in a game, blown it on a trip, forgotten it.

A private detective had been summoned to appear; he had once been hired by a casino to dig up what he could on the couple. He consulted his yellowed notes, a treasury tag rusted into them, to state that he had pinned the woman down to Chisinau, or Kishinev, Moldova, or Moldavia, a confusion of names reflecting the subjugation of a place, it seemed, that was always getting in the way: Bessarabia. The word drew more puzzled glances from around the room. The detective had begun to weary of the question 'Where?' It was a backwater up near Russia that was home to some unremarkable people until avaricious powers set their dark hearts on it, and that was the only way he felt he could explain it. He could safely offer Romania as the woman's place of origin, he said. In a way, it hardly mattered, as she spoke perfect French, and was surprised and, he remembered, quite frosty, if anybody referred to her origins.

She had been ill for some time, a neighbor testified.

"How ill?" a court officer asked.

"She was taking… medicine."

The neighbor's gaze rested somewhat mercilessly on Henri. He seemed oblivious as fifty faces turned towards him, sat there as he was, thinking, they were fine when I left them – they were fine, they really were.

Madame Luciana, a skinny thing to begin with, had lost a lot of weight very quickly, the neighbor continued, had eaten next to nothing, not even the little Greek cakes she had brought over at Easter, which, everybody agreed, were irresistible – she had been told so, many times. "Thank you," the court officer had said, hurriedly. It wasn't beyond the bounds of belief, then, that the woman had died of that not-so-mysterious illness, exacerbated by a plunge into the cold water of a poisoned little lake? The neighbor regretted finding herself in reluctant agreement.

The detective was called again to declare that the man had been an Armenian. He too had rarely discussed his origins, but he had looked like an Armenian – like Charles Aznavour, in fact, it was pointed out. Indeed, some years before, he had been convicted for impersonating Mr. Aznavour in several fancy hotels along the coast and running up sizeable bills, sent to Mr. Aznavour's agent. Twice. His surname had an Armenian ending, though his nationality was French.

"Was he sick, too?" The question went around the court.

"He was… old," somebody said.

"I'm old," the coroner said. The gallery laughed, and the court's officers, unsure of the freedom to follow, hid their laughter in their hands. "Let's leave it that it's not age alone that kills, and that's what we're here to determine."

"He was frail," Anina Delessena testified. "And, it seemed to me, very suddenly." There she was, called again, rising to her full meter-and-a-half height again, stating, once again, her disgruntlement at the lack of a Bible on which to swear. "One minute it seemed as if he was about to break into a tango." This was greeted with some laughter. Anina Delessena frowned, looked over the room, then perhaps saw the comic absurdity in it, and gave in, and smiled. "He was a very good dancer," she explained. "In his time. But no more. I think he lost his…

spark, his dynamo, very suddenly – overnight. He was worried about his wife, I think."

"That could prove fatal," the coroner agreed drily. He looked pointedly at his watch, which immediately made everybody think of lunch, and hurriedly pronounced his verdict.

Twenty Three

Foul play was dismissed, but still that verdict was open, as was the aperture in the fence supposed to keep tippers out of the dump. As soon as the municipality had fixed it, some enterprising rogue had cut the fence again, in two places.

After the funeral, Henri stood beside it. He had seen the tippers at work, and knew he could get in. He pushed at the fence with a foot, and made it open wide enough to allow him through. He stepped in, and at once felt a shiver of disquiet.

He walked carefully a little way out, and glanced up at the windows of the apartment over the car service place. He guessed that both Armen and Luciana had, just about, been able to see the tippers come in, laden, and out, their hands free.

There was no reason for Armen and Luciana to have gone through that fence, Henri kept saying to himself. He took a few more paces. The slope gained its angle almost immediately. The crimson sofa he had seen two men pull through the fence only the day before was waterlogged, and perhaps fifteen meters down. He took a few steps, and his feet felt lighter, and tighter, his toes in his shoes struggling for a foothold, a feeling at the base of his skull and in his guts telling him that the earth was moving beneath him – a strange, unsettling feeling – and that his balance was about to be compromised. He stood still, found his equilibrium in his own time. He looked across the dump, down at the toxic water at the bottom.

No reason for them to go in there, to do that fatal last tango. What was it they'd said, that it was better to have a mystery than to solve one? No, that really wasn't true. He pondered the few words for what seemed like hours.

He hadn't watched the bodies being recovered. He hadn't wanted to. There had been frogmen, he had heard – he had almost laughed at the way this child's picture of the divers had made its way into everyday speech and lingered there. There had been winches borrowed from the mountain rescue services, apparently, long chains paid out by a truck anchored by weights back up on the road. There had been a crowd, muted gossiping, sad shakes of the head.

He had seen people gathering, and had stopped. He had turned, and gone back into Nice. He had sought out oblivion among the new friends he was busy cultivating, none of whom would ever draw a crowd, he reflected, none of whom would be worth it, nor remembered with anything but a slight wrinkling of the nose.

The crowd gone, the tippers absent, and not even a dog in sight, Henri felt oppressed by the loneliness of the scene before him. He felt it was a shame, no, a tragedy – and a puzzling one, that left him feeling helpless and angry – that Armen and Luciana should have ended their days in such a ruinous and terrible place.

Henri stood there. When he looked around him, the night had started to bring its dark blue. He took a step, and his ankle twisted, and he nearly lost his balance. He raised his hands, trying to stabilize it. He dared another step, and this time felt the ground shift. His breath turned into a yelp as his arm was grabbed from behind him.

Emilie Brun said nothing as she pulled at Henri's arm. She dragged him up a few steps, and watched as he came to a rest. That was all it took, they were both thinking: just one unwise step onto a patch of loose detritus, and they would have been falling, sinking.

"You scared me." Henri tried not to make it sound like a complaint. She laughed lightly anyway.

She had dropped a bunch of flowers in giving her attentions to Henri. She stepped to them carefully, and retrieved them.

"You saved me," he said. Several times, he thought he remembered, later. They were both trembling. He remembered that.

She said, "Come on," and nodded up the slope to the road.

She pulled the ribbon and tissue paper off the flowers, separated them, and scattered them as she walked carefully back up the slope, marking their trail with them.

Twenty Four

She would move, Emilie decided, to the other side of the city. Henri, who kept to no side of anywhere he had ever been, saw that the decision had made her happy. He sensed the words before she ever uttered them: she would move away with her man.

She had grown to like Henri a little when he had come to the apartment and sat in the corner, made his enigmatic smile, and to like him a lot when he had stayed with Anina, and had given up his day-to-day life – whatever form that might ever have taken – to the search for Armen and Luciana. When they still had a mystery to solve, Henri had worn out his shoes all over Nice and beyond to ask questions of everybody and anybody. His doggedness in the face of both sympathy and apathy, and the occasional threat, had been admirable, but his acts of avoidance, once it was plain that the couple were lost, were those of a man unable to face the real things in life, Emilie had told him frankly.

Out of the blue, Henri had gone to her, all groomed, and looking almost straight, though she had giggled when she looked down and saw flecks of toothpaste on his shoes. His rambling speech had ended with a fumble in a complicated-looking system of pockets-within-pockets, and the offer of a gold ring in need of a polish. She had stared pointedly at it, and Henri had had to digress to own up to having borrowed it from the small box of rings Armen and Luciana had accepted in lieu of winnings, or abandoned IOUs.

Henri had dived further into digression, and called to words Luciana's story about having lost her own ring out on the dump: a row, and an impulsive throw. It kept coming back to puzzle him. He sometimes wondered if it was just a sentimental lie, and she had actually lost it in a game, the couple having hit true rock-bottom. That was the night he'd first heard of genocide, he remembered, first-hand, and not from Pathé News, the cinema after the war, and the camera roving pitilessly over the Jews' stuff all piled together, shoes, glasses, suitcases, hair, for Christ's sake – hair – and rings, thousands of rings. A ring had been embedded into the flesh of Luciana's ring finger when she was found – one from the box, he assumed. They couldn't have wandered out there in search of her lost ring, could they... and if so, if some mad urge had really taken them down there, they couldn't have found it... could they?

"No." Emilie bit her lip, shook her head, glad, for the moment, of the diversion. Henri was staring into the distance, shaking his head, the ring still clutched absurdly between thumb and finger. "Of course not."

She had reluctantly prodded him back into his interrupted proposal, and he had resumed his babbling. She had thought it best to let it peter out, guiding it into nothingness with nods that revealed, somewhat paradoxically, her refusal. Though she had grown to like Henri, she had decided with some regret that she would never be able to trust him. She saw the methadone in his eyes – a sign of improvement, she understood, but not a big enough one to matter – and had to lower her own eyes, and take his hand, and shake it, and thank him, and promise that she would always think of him in fondness.

She let him know as gently as she could that her future lay elsewhere, with the blue-eyed wavy-haired flic who'd laughed at her jokes and paid her compliments. He had also magicked away a fine incurred by her careless parking of Bill Wyman's car, increased by its temporary disappearance aided by the fact that she couldn't remember where she'd left it. That had been a busy, crowded night, after all. He had also facilitated the red-tape-free return of Mr. Wyman's car with the hope that he would get the fullest satisfaction from being reunited with it. That part of the story allowed Henri to laugh a little, and he was still smiling as he walked down the stairs of the block, away from kindly Emilie Brun for the last time.

Twenty Five

He thought he saw it all, in moments of half-dream between wakefulness and sleep: a walk in the dark, a power cut, a wrong turning, the howl of a trapped dog on the dump, an act of foolish kindness – impulsive, ridiculous, the audacious part of their nature eclipsing the cautious side for a few crucial seconds. "How else could it have been?" he began to ask Jules, and Anina Delessena, and some of his new friends in the Arab quarter, and in the bars near the station. They didn't know – nobody knew, and nobody ever would.

They had learned the trick of forgetting the bad, Henri saw at last. Their lives had been full of it – so much of it. They had to forget it, or they'd dwell on it forever, and be brought down by it, ruined, would disappear into it. Henri resolved to learn the trick of forgetting.

He never quite managed it, but only once in a while found himself staring at puddles, thinking of Armen's escape from Smyrna. That man had spent more than enough time in dirty water, more than any man deserved in any lifetime. A shame.

He sometimes let his mopey walks take him down to that characterless suburb of Nice with its blocks and its garage and its dump. He often found himself standing at the gap in the fence. At dusk, and everybody home from work, the water hammers would start up in the apartments nearby, and Henri would think of the pipes, feeding that foul pond below. He thought of the rain, too, and would look up, see it darken the sky, the bay suddenly devoid of angels. The only splash of color would arrive in the form of two yellow planes, which circled in what looked to be lazy contentment, before their pilots were satisfied that all was well on the Blue Coast, and made their way on home.

Twenty Six

I don't think I'll ever go to Nice. I'm not sure why. At one time, I was curious about the places Henri talked about, but I'm not, anymore. There's something about them I no longer like the sound of. Perhaps it's all those lives ruined by greed, or all those spoilt countesses and film and rock stars trapped in their mansions and their aimlessness, those refugees not knowing what they're after in a place like that till they find it and hate it but are stuck with it, and all those broken people, like Henri. I suppose London must be the same, or worse, for those people, but I don't see it, because I'm part of the background. I don't think of the damaged people till I see them come in the door of St. Giles, under their own steam or propelled, horizontally.

It would kill me to see those little yellow planes over Nice and the coast in search of flash fires and smugglers, but finding the results of misadventure, those who'd run out of even the worst kind of luck. I would think of Armen and Luciana, and of Henri himself, and it would be like listening to a sad song over and over again.

On a whim, I bought that album the Stones recorded in the basement of Keith Richards' mansion at Villefranche. It wasn't my kind of music, to be honest. I was slightly shocked that it was so bluesy; it wasn't even pop. I expected it to at least have some flavor of the Blue Coast to it, but there was none, no hint of those places Henri told me about, those roads up and down the coast, the casinos, the people around the Bay of Angels. And of course, it told me nothing, because it's people who tell stories, and much better than even the most expressive music. Even the Stones, their taxes paid or successfully avoided, presumably, forgot their exile and that album, and the stories on it are out there still, forgotten too, though hidden in plain sight.

When people disappear, their stories go with them, unless somebody keeps them alive, somehow. It was a great thing, I thought, that Henri had brought his friends' stories with him. I'd never heard of Armenia until I met Henri, never heard of Bessarabia, or however people choose to call it now, nor Smyrna, never heard of genocide, didn't know people could be so cruel, or so kind.

As for the bearer of these tales, I often had an eye half-open for him in Camberwell, a little of my bleary gaze saved for him if it was the morning. He affected not to see me once, and I was slightly annoyed. Later, I assumed he did it out of courtesy, to protect me from some nearby company he was keeping, or from himself, even, one of the impenetrable moods that kidnapped him sometimes, or just a bad smell he was giving off. What else did he have to hide, somebody as open as Henri? I won't say the question kept occurring to me, but it was sometimes half-formed before I dismissed it. I repaid him by pretending I couldn't see him once – I forget why. I just wasn't in the mood, I suppose.

So Henri was around, part of my background. Then he wasn't. I realized that I'd not seen him for a month, then two, then three. It didn't matter, not... really. I was twenty by then, was in turn frivolous, and just stupid, sometimes, still captured by the light-hearted preoccupations of my teens, but serious, too, studious when I had to be, and diligent at work, and sometimes in love very suddenly and, just as suddenly, out of it.

I got drunk in The Orange Tree pub once, and convinced myself that I had to find Henri, that very minute. It was some time after last orders. I got ooh-la-las from my friends. "No," I assured them. "He's this... bloke from work. He's a..."

"Doctor," they said, and laughed, and one made a joke about his cold hands and stethoscope on my chest.

I said, "No – no. He's..." And I remember them all looking at me, and then at one another. "Going to tell me some more... stories," I said. I walked out into the night, in search of Henri and his tales. I was finally diverted home by my amused friends, convincing me that some bloke from work, and some patient – not a doctor, not even a porter – didn't matter on a summer Saturday night when you could walk through the streets of Camberwell, singing the number one song at the time, badly, and with comic vibrato, Charles Aznavour's She.

But then Henri's absence did matter, sometimes, and it had a great weight, and fell on me, for no good reason. When it did, I plucked up the courage to ask men of Henri's kind in Camberwell Green if they'd seen him. I asked other nurses at St. Giles. I asked Nick, the owner of the café we had sometimes gone to. He made a show of thinking, almost ending with a nod, but all it signified was that he knew who I meant, and finally he shook his head in both disapproval and regret. Nick the Camberwell Greek, I recall thinking, not a Blue Coast Greek, like Anina Delessena, nor an Asia Minor Greek, like the doomed priests and merchants of Smyrna.

If Henri was really gone, I could only guess at his fate. I checked the space-filling three-line reports of small tragedies in the South London Press, to see if Henri could matter enough to merit one. He wasn't there among the acts of violence or not-worth-it theft, the instances of drunken affray, the revelation of bodies neglected till they were discovered. I probably missed a few. If some bad, or just careless, act had put an end to Henri, I wanted to know. I wanted the impossible: to complete his story.

My alarm clock roused me into a panic one morning, and I got halfway out of bed before I remembered it was a day off. As I settled back down, relieved but grumpy, I had a sharply-cut picture of Henri in Armen and Luciana's apartment over the garage in Nice, though, puzzlingly, it wasn't exactly how he'd pictured it for me. He stayed there for a while, I remembered, during the interval between the vanishing of his friends and their death. I suppose he'd harbored a deluded hope that they'd make a spectacular comeback, and had watched the street, and the path outside, hoping to see his delicate friends making a dainty way through the scattered parts of cars kept by old Villemont in his own deluded hope of turning a small profit on them.

It may not be obvious, but I must confess here that I didn't always listen very carefully to Henri. At his most earnest, I realized later, he wasn't bothered about that; it was more important for him to speak than it was to be heard. Our conversations often took place in less than ideal conditions, too, on noisy Camberwell Green or on a corner nearby, the roar of traffic breaking them up, or amid the thrum of chatter and the clatter of plates in Nick's Café, or, at St. Giles, in the common room under a telly turned to blaring for the hard-of-hearing, and alongside the demands of other patients. Some of the conversations came back to me from time to time, when a lingering fragment would suddenly make sense, and for no logical reason: I'd hear a word, or read one, see a picture, in front of me or in my mind, and a connection would spark into life. The morning I lost my day off lie-in, I recalled Henri talking about a flat – not an apartment, in the French parlance – and it wasn't the yellow one over Villemont's garage, but a different one. I couldn't help but picture it as a sordid little bolt-hole, with dusty doilies on shabby furniture, the kind of touch a clueless man from another time would think a woman might like. It would be good enough, just about, for a mistress, a one-time secretary, or – I shouldn't be snobby – a nurse, even, who'd been kind to a civil servant who was no good at cards. I always imagined a man in a creaseless mac, belted fastidiously around his waist, and a bowler hat, a brolly in one hand, a briefcase in the other, to guard against the rain and the flying away of mundane official secrets. I saw the flat he lost to Armen and Luciana as the kind of place that might suit Henri; after all, any flat was better than the open and its unpredictable denizens, and the elements – even better, probably, than St. Giles.

The last occasion I'd seen Henri kept coming back from the haze into which it had settled in my mind, like a barely remembered telly advert that was annoying and yet, somehow, fascinating. I remembered that I was on Camberwell Church Street near the library, just passing, on the way to the bus stop. Henri was across the busy street, in front of the police station. I knew his form as well as I knew anybody's, just from seeing it in the corner of my eye, like I would, say, a public figure or one in the news. He was unmistakable. I didn't quite stop, as I had an evening class to get to at Goldsmith's, up the road in New Cross, and I was running late, but I waved. He widened his eyes in recognition. I saw his arm twitch, the start of a wave in return. A bus drew up both on my side of the road and on his. They slowed down for a matter of perhaps ten seconds, for the hesitant amber of traffic lights, but were gone quickly enough for me to be expecting to see Henri, revealed, and approaching. I didn't. It was as if he'd emulated his Blue Coast friends and disappeared on the spot. He may have boarded the bus on his side, of course, jumped on the platform, but it had barely stopped, and, while not exactly decrepit, he really wouldn't have been quite nimble enough.

There was a dry cleaner's next to the police station – the 1940 Dry Cleaners – and an off-license. I crossed the road, and looked in both. The offy had only one customer, a teen looking nervous about his purchase – trying too hard to look grown-up, as I'd done myself, many a time, and in that very same establishment. The cleaner's was closed, though a middle-aged woman was in there, discontentedly mopping the floor. She paused, peered at me momentarily over her glasses, then got back to work. But no Henri.

I'd see him again, I supposed. I never did.

When you read a book or watch a series on the telly, there is always a ray of hope that one of your favorite characters can make a spectacular comeback from a disappearance, even from a death. I wondered if Henri might. The end of his misadventures may have been a sure thing, whether in some hospital ward – and why not mine? Not good enough anymore, I wondered – or in a needle-strewn alley or squat, or simply in winter sunshine on an unforgiving iron bench on Camberwell Green among stupefied members of his tribe.

I'd stopped searching the South London Press's little tragedies, however, once the idea hit me that Henri had blagged the London flat he had sometimes talked about – the one Armen and Luciana had won from that hapless civil servant on his holiday and off his game. Once it occurred to me, I could never quite dismiss the idea. It would have been nothing as ordered as their having made a will, or got a lawyer to pass Henri a set of deeds – of course not. He had simply acquired them, when, bereft of his countess, he'd stayed in Armen and Luciana's apartment to wait for his friends to reappear from the ether around him, a vigil in genuine hope that they'd walk across that yard and up those stairs.

I remembered his confessions of despondency at times, and of his dopey stupors and opiate dreams. I imagined him reassuring Emilie Brun, and Anina Delessena, and Villemont the mechanic and Adie, the landlord, and any other interested parties, that he would keep the place aired for Armen and Luciana until their return. I guessed that he'd had himself a bit of a rummage to fill in those empty hours of heroin and methadone and waiting, and thinking of ways to woo the unsuspecting Emilie Brun – had a rummage, found all but meaningless documents and, among them, black and stark or shiny and barely used, keys that would open locked doors in a run-down part of London, to reveal a gloomy, pokey little flat where only sad things had happened. He had confessed to having helped himself to one of his friends' small collection of rings suitable to woo Blue Coast hairdressers. So why not the keys?

Once it became clear that he would never see his friends again, it was clear too that the London flat was not going to be any use to anybody – they had no heirs, of course, and no wills in any case. He had given up on his attempt to win Emilie's heart, so there was nothing for it but to give up too on the Blue Coast. He had headed home – not to Boston, of course. I'd asked him why London, why South London, and why Camberwell, and he'd offered me a cheerful why not; it was as good a place as any to lead a quiet life, another life, free of at least some of his past mistakes.

I try not to think about Henri. I try, but, if I'm around the Green, I can't help but almost come to a stop if a hangdog figure shuffles into the picture, hoping it's him, and hoping it's not. Often when I pass, it's as if my feet won't let me hurry by, and of their own accord make me stand by the library on Church Street, opposite the 1940 Dry Cleaner's. I note the drinkers heading left, to the Merlin's Cave, I suppose, and right, to the Tiger. I note the wet-haired kids out of the swimming baths, to my left, clutching their bags of chips, voices loud, shrill, harsh. I note the crowds of yobs in blue-and-white scarves on Millwall home days, headed up to New Cross, though not to Goldsmith's. I note the vagrants, headed for the Green to live their pitiable lives in public, and yet also to become a part of the backdrop, ghostly, and almost invisible.

It all prompts me to wonder if Armen and Luciana mentioned the local landmarks when they recounted details of their visit to their gloomy new property: the Salvation Army HQ crowning the hill, perhaps, the Maudsley Hospital for the Insane, or the Fox on the Hill pub, or the Tiger, though, to be honest, I can't picture Armen or Luciana in any of them. I'm intrigued that my mum, who had worked in the Tiger since records began, the seventy eight RPM kind, might have served the genteel Blue Coast couple, Armen with a pernod, perhaps, Luciana with a… what? White wine? Did the

Tiger even have those? The thought of Armen and Luciana wandering into the Tiger is kind of mad… but perhaps just as mad as the thought of Henri wandering down the Promenade des Anglais among the flâneurs and boulevardiers.

I also wonder sometimes how Henri could bear to spend his days in Camberwell; I mean… after the Blue Coast, and the Stones, and all, and meeting people from places that no longer existed, and eyewitnesses' recounting of genocide, not forgetting drives in a rock star's car. I think I asked him once, and I seem to remember that he laughed at the spurious nature of the question, or at its mundanity. It seems to me that, just as Henri didn't deem his early life in Boston-not-the-one-in-Massachusetts worthy of recounting, his time in Camberwell was to be consigned to similar shadows. His real life, his only life, had been on the Blue Coast, and he had lived it, and it was done. Perhaps it was that simple to him.

Sometimes, just for the sake of it, I come to a halt on Church Street. I look up at the dark windows above the 1940 Cleaner's, and the offy, over the police station. I imagine Henri behind those grubby curtains, abandoned to a kind of narcolepsy, a parallel life of it, on hold until he gets down to the sun again, gets himself a new countess, and a rock star's car, and a chauffeur, too, and makes himself some exotic new friends.

Acknowledgments

I couldn't have written this without the unfailing help and support of my wife, Jacqueline Sweeney, who accompanied me to the Blue Coast and drove me up and down its hills and along its boulevards while I ruminated on its stories, and to Armenia, where the good people we met put the final story into my mind. She also wrote words of wisdom over early drafts in her elegant hand.

Paul Lyon brought his merciless and unfailing eye for a good sentence to all of them in this book. There are a few missing in action, that Paul assured me I wouldn't want back.

My mother Mrs. Frances Sweeney brought me on my first ever trip into Camberwell's St. Giles hospital, starting the whole thing off. She was a kindly nurse with a distracted ear for the stories I told – which were not very good at the time. As she was never afraid of hard work, she also pulled the odd pint in The Tiger pub when times were hard.